# Table of Contents

# INTRODUCTION

I grew up in a family where story telling was a tradition.  We heard stories all the time.  It didn't matter what season; how hot or how cold, when any of these yarns were told, they were told on our front porch with either a glass of sweet tea, or a warm mug of hot chocolate with marshmallows.

I guess this sort of made it all the more special. All of us kids, adults, and neighbors gathered on my parent's porch; a beautiful night sky, listening to someone tell a story.  This was a part of my childhood that I cherished.  It is the reason that I came up with the idea, and wrote a collection of short stories that could be spoken and enjoyed from the front porch.

Stories from the Front Porch are a collection of five short stories with a wide range of stories ranging from: mysteries, love, friendship, male bonding, and overcoming incredible odds.  Stories from the Front Porch are an assortment of simple feel good narratives with universal appeal.  Women, men, young and seasoned readers will enjoy the diverse variety through a shared experience or an intimate setting on the front porch alone reading.

Maybe it's just me, but the art of story-telling has long diminished.  Gone are the days of gathering around a radio, and a front porch to hear a tale from an elder mostly regarding an event that really happened and changed their lives in some aspect. Through this series, I hope to bring this lost art back because it brings families together, gives parents the chance to bond and it unites communities together in a very unique and special way.

My hope for this series is to simply bring enjoyment and a quiet reflection of simpler times where good old fashion story-telling was appreciated and provide story-tellers as well as those of us who just enjoy a great story with a joyous experience. Happy reading.

I0537528

## Conversations Amongst Women

It was odd how we met; the corner Starbucks on Melbourne Street.  Mrs. Brooks was an older African American woman who wore pretty sun dresses and hats.  Every afternoon she'd sway into the Starbucks on Melbourne order a slice of banana nut bread, and a slice of pumpkin bread with a caramel latte.  Lydia, my older sister noticed Mrs. Brooks first. It had to be her hats that got Lydia's attention.

The hats said a lot about her.  She wore many, each telling their own unique story of her life.  The hat she was wearing today spoke the language of spring. It was a golden yellow with beautiful wildflowers and tulips forming from the side of her hat.  On the right side of her hat were tiny trees, and a birds nest with three small brown eggs laying comfortable waiting to be hatched.

My favorite was the pink one. It showcased a petite rose garden with white and yellow flowers woven in between. Like the yellow hat, the right side of the pink one had an empty row of cracked ground with a lonely stock of wheat in it that had grown wild. It was an interesting hat to say the least. For some odd reason, it spoke to me. It displayed both beauty and both ashes. I don't know why we paid so much attention to her hats. May be it was because they told stories?

Sometimes I wondered what stories that we told her? Or, if we communicated anything at all to her? The Starbucks on Melbourne was a place for Lydia and me to just breathe, and let our hair down before we went home to screaming kids jumping up on their mommies, and too many of them all trying to tell mommy something at once, and husbands that loved us and cooked for us, but left the kitchen a mess.

Blair would be in my ear about the upcoming Pre-season football schedule as well as the season opener, and all the home games that he wanted me and the kids to attend. And Marcus would be giving Lydia a short notice on a dinner party to impress the President of MSNBC.

Lydia and I shared everything; everything, and Starbucks was the place for us to share it. No kids, no husbands, none of our employees over hearing our dirty little secrets that only sisters could laugh about and appreciate. Our booth was in the corner by the big double doors, overlooking tall green mountains and botanic gardens decorated with beauty. We saw everyone who came in, and everyone who went out; which is how we began seeing Mrs. Brooks and the stunning hats she wore.

"Spring," Lydia tapped me on the hand and tilted her head over towards the front counter.

"Isn't that Mason Cunningham, Hill's husband with ole girl at the front counter?" Lydia said.

I sipped my latte and bit into my pumpkin bread, and slightly turned my head. "What?" I was shocked. "He is dipping for real." I said. "You think she knows?" I carefully watched them.

"What woman doesn't?" Lydia took a bite of her banana bread.

"I feel like going over there." I said.

"Yeah me too," Lydia said. "But he'd make it to her first and lie, and you know her, she'd believe him."

"That's a shame, but that's the truth, and then we'd have to cuss her out." I said, sipping my latte.

"I can't believe he's going to sit here with that woman like she's his? That's some nerve." Lydia said.

"It is his." I said, making that experience woman face women make when men and life teach them lessons.

Lydia burst out laughing. I don't know what I said that was so funny. I guess sometimes the truth is funny. In a weird way, Lydia's laughing had gotten Mason's attention. He saw both of us. The look on his face was priceless. And, he damn near choked on his coffee.

Like he was on a track scholarship, he bolted and left "other woman" sitting right there. It was a sight to see her ask the back side of him all kinds of questions he would never answer. She of course ran out after him and the coward that he was drove off and left her. Mrs. Brooks even laughed. Somehow our eyes met. The way women's eyes meet when Juicy stuff, like secret Starbucks affairs go down.

She didn't know Mason or "other woman," like we did. But, she didn't have to. She was a woman who knew women like "other woman," and Mrs. Brooks had stories herself. Her hats told us so. Mrs. Brooks tossed her plate in the trash. She looked over at me and Lydia and laughed.

"Did you all see that?" She said, shaking her head.

"Yeah," Lydia said. "No good son of a..."

"Lydia," I said.

"Well, you know he ain't no good girl." My sister said. "You saw him."

Mrs. Brooks paused. "Y'all know him.

"Yes, unfortunately," I said.

"Uh-oh," she said. "Mind if I sit?" Mrs. Brooks said.

Lydia scooted over and Mrs. Brooks sat and that was it. The bond between us formed quickly.

The booth that once sat two, now sat three. Every afternoon between one and two o'clock, the three of us met and shared our stories: love, laughter, loss, pain, and secrets.

"Now you know that's something," Mrs. Brooks said.

"True," Lydia agreed. "But, let's just put it out there." She said. "Hill knew what she was getting into. She had to have him."

"Um-hum," I said, "following him around like some love struck puppy dog."

"Humph!" Mrs. Brooks said. "I know one thing. He's a looker, and that car he flew off in, sure was nice. What kind of work does he do?" She asked.

"Pro basketball player with the Portland Trail Blazers," I said.

Chile," she tossed her hand. "I don't know nothing about no sports honey." She laughed.

"But I do know about some love, celebration, and pain." She said, as her jubilant demeanor suddenly changed, then turned joyful again.

Lydia and I looked at each other. We knew those hats she wore were clusters of stories that laid a foundation of who Mrs. Brooks really was. She tilted her hat to the side where we could see the birds nest and the three brown eggs in it. An attractive hat but what did it mean?

"My first husband bought me this hat after our youngest baby girl graduated from high school." She said. "Girls," she laughed. "I fell in love with it like I had fallen madly in love with him." She smiled. "The three eggs represent our three children, and now our three grandchildren." She sighed remembering.

Oh," she stared off into space. "Those wore the good old days. The days of love, family, big old Sunday meals after church, big barbeques all summer long, and loving girls, good loving." She paused. "Oh, life was so good to me then." She said. "Enough about me, tell me about the two of you."

"Well," Lydia cleared her throat. "I'm Lydia the older sister. I've been married for ten years. We have four beautiful daughters, and I own several restaurants, and my husband is a broadcaster for MSNBC."

"Well you just go right ahead Mrs. Thing," Mrs. Brooks smiled, turning her attention to me.

"My husband and I have twins; Hezekiah and Charity." I smiled. I always smiled when I mentioned my kids because I knew that they were gifts to me. "They're great kids and I love them, but ..." I laughed.

"Baby," Mrs. Brooks said. "That's why they call them kids."

Before she could ask, I told her about Blair, the love of my life who had me autograph a book for his aunt at one of my book signings; then stood in line a second time for me to autograph a book for an uncle, a brother, and friend, after that I stopped counting. We had our first cup of coffee at the Starbucks on Melbourne Street. So, I guess I could say that this Starbucks does have sentimental value.

I told her that my Blair is a pro football player with two super bowl rings, two amazing twins, and two adorable German Shepherd's; yet he wants two more kids. I love him hard. But, when I say that I'm done having kids, he just kisses me and says naughty things in my ear.

"Girl," Mrs. Brooks laughed. "You had better watch that man. You'll be peeing on a stick and eating bland soda crackers for long."

"I'm on the pill." I blurted it out, but he doesn't know it. I feel bad that I'm lying to him. But,"

Lydia and Mrs. Brooks laughed hard. I laughed to. It was a bonding laugh; a laugh between women and sisters where we knew our secrets were safe. I looked at Lydia briefly. She was me when I would become older; beautiful, seasoned.

Lydia loved her restaurants. She was there every day. But on Sunday's, all of them were closed. We were raised to honor the Sabbath and we did. We honored it with love and big Sunday dinner's alternating houses in which we cooked. It was convenient. Lydia and I lived right next door to each other. We planned it that way, and it worked out perfect.

Marcus had been at Lydia to relax more, and not spend so much time at her restaurants.

He wanted to spend more time with her and their girls. He had altered his schedule at the studio after his girls were born and had fallen into a position that he absolutely loved. They had a beautiful vacation home in Maui, and Marcus to wanted another baby. Lydia was fine with having another baby, but it was just tying her down long enough to have one. She had given him a date of when she would just let her GM's take over, and that date was approaching. But, Lydia had fibbed to my brother-in-law, and told him one of her restaurants was in trouble.

Mrs. Brooks laughed again. "Humph!" She said. "Y'all is some lying heifers. But, I can't say nothing," she said. "I cheated on mines with my college sweetheart."

For a moment, there was that jaw dropping look between my sister and I. We couldn't believe what we were hearing.  If looks defined acts of cheating, which they don't, we would have never guessed that Mrs. Brooks had cheated on her husband.  And, who would guess that I was lying to mines, and that Lydia was lying to hers.  Now, I felt guiltier.  I wondered if Lydia did?

"Did he ever find out?"  I asked.

"Yeah he did," she said, with a sad look in her eyes.  "He never forgave me after that.  He said he did, but he didn't.  I could tell."  Her eyes watered. "He didn't love me the same; didn't hold me the same, didn't kiss me the same," tears leaked from her eyes.

"I'm so sorry."  I said.

Me too," Lydia echoed behind me.

"I think he stayed with me to punish me."  She said.

"He had to love you a lot to stay."  Lydia said.

"No," she said with a half-smile. "You know what I did?"

"No," we said.

"I went to the boutique and bought me a pretty pink hat. I'm sure you've seen it. The one with the pretty pink rose garden with beautiful white and yellow roses." She said. "The garden was our life together. The white flowers stood for the purity in our relationship, and the yellow ones, our friendship." Tears formed again in her eyes. "He was my lover; my best friend and I blew it on some school girl heat between my legs." She cried.

Lydia took one hand and I took other. Mrs. Brooks just wept; wept sore. It broke my heart and Lydia's to. Before we knew it, we were all crying, sharing Mrs. Brooks pain and claiming it as our own. I always knew there was a story behind her hats.

Now, without her saying anything more about the cracked ground, or the tall single stock of wheat standing in an empty row, I knew.

Plan and simple, her life had started in the spring, and died miserably in the winter. She was broken, and we could see that she had many regrets. She looked at us, held our hands tight and squeezed them, and slowly we could see spring return to her eyes again.

"My Benny's gone now." She wiped her tears. "And do you know he left me everything, everything, but, that's the kind of person he was." She shook her head. "He made me promise not to tell our daughter's. He said it wasn't for them to know." She blew her nose. "Do you think that's right?"

"What's your heart telling you?" Lydia said.

"Of course I don't want them to know," she said. "I'm so ashamed. But, I don't want to hurt them like

I hurt their father. I've lied enough, but I'm afraid."

"Forgive yourself." I said. "And once you can look in the mirror and love yourself in spite of, go from there." I squeezed her hand. "Your heart will decide if they need to know or not." I said.

"Well," she said, with a more joyous disposition. "That's about the best damn advice I've had." She smiled.

Lydia and I looked at each other. I could see that she was thinking about Marcus, and I was thinking about Blair. We both loved Starbucks for the simple joy of getting away and sharing. I didn't want to be Mrs. Brooks in twenty years, telling some younger woman how I lied to Blair and he walked. Lydia didn't want to be in Maui alone staring out at the beautiful ocean side without Marcus.

I looked at my watch and it was exactly two o'clock. We hugged Mrs. Brooks, switched phone numbers, and addresses. Weeks later the three of us were back at the same booth talking, laughing, and laughing more at me. I had flat out lied to my husband about being on birth control. But despite my efforts, the joke was on me. I had gotten pregnant anyway.

When I told Mrs. Brooks she laughed hard. Somehow we all laughed real hard until we cried. But, it was a good cry loaded with joyful tears. We still talked girl talk; still divulged secrets, but today at the Starbucks on Melbourne Street, we were planning my baby shower.

The End

# A Presences at the Lake

It was supposed to be the best summer of our lives. My parents were finally taking their Caribbean vacation. And Jamaal and I were all excited. They wanted to go long before we were born. But apparently, money was tight, and as they put it, there were other priorities that came first like rent, bills, and saving for the home that Jamaal and I grew up in. They were going to be gone for a month, thanks to Grandpa Ezekiel, My brother Jamaal and I was headed to Copper Springs with him. We were both in trouble and Grandpa promised to whip us both back into shape. Actually, he had sat aside chores for us to do; hard chores, chores that taught you something, and made you think twice about putting blue lizards down Gretchen McCall's back.

Gretchen McCall was ten, medium height, soft brown skin, and rich. Her mother was the District Attorney in Citrus Grove, California where we lived. And her father was some big shot doctor that put people to sleep during surgery. She had everything she wanted plus. Every year she went to some part of Europe for summer vacation. Gretchen even spoke French. This year she and her parents were going to the French Riviera, and of course she bragged to all the neighborhood kids about it. I hated her. Not because she was rich, but because she always poked fun at me because we weren't.

Mama was a college professor at the University. Daddy was a Chemical Engineer. They were doing alright I guess? We didn't go on fancy vacations in the summer. We didn't get new cars every other year, and Jamaal or I didn't go to private school, or have a chauffeur take us. We went to public school like all the other kids in our neighborhood; everybody except Gretchen.

It wasn't my idea. I swear. It was my brother Jamaal's. Gretchen had made fun of our bikes. She bragged about her father's new Mercedes, and she poked fun at me wearing overalls and baseball caps. She said it loud to my face, in front of all the neighborhood kids, that I had as much looks to me as a moose wearing lipstick. Her words cut me hard and cold. Like the skinny nine year old kid I was then, I ran as fast as I could home, shot up the stairs, and fell on my bed sobbing.

That was it. That was all it took for Jamaal to seek revenge on Gretchen. He could poke fun at me all day. But to his credit, he never made me cry. If he saw that I was on the verge, he'd stop, make stupid faces, and make me charge after him. He hated to see me cry. I don't know why, he just did. He promised an ice cream cone dipped in chocolate, and two books: Heidi and The Three Musketeers if I'd help him catch a blue lizard and put it down the back of Gretchen's dress. That's how we got in trouble, got grounded, and almost got sent to Aunt Zoe's house instead of Copper Springs.

Aunt Zoe was a shopaholic. And, it didn't help that she lived in New York, Manhattan at that. We'd shop with her for two days straight, and for a week, we'd turn New York inside out. Aunt Zoe was fun, but spontaneous, and her spontaneity drove both Jamaal and I nuts at times. One time in the middle of dinner at a fancy restaurant, Aunt Zoe paid for our half eaten meals, and left a whopping tip. Before we could blink, she had whisked us onto her private plane, flew us to San Francisco to hang out with her boyfriend that played for the San Francisco Giants.

We never knew what to expect from Aunt Zoe. Neither did mama, Aunt Zoe was always, always a last resort. She was loaded and she was a free spirit, and it drove mama crazy to.

Whenever we did visit Aunt Zoe, it was wild, and fun. Jamaal and I always returned home with expensive clothes and shoes and delicious chocolate chip cookies. Aunt Zoe couldn't cook worth squat but she made the best chocolate chip cookies ever.

It was a three hour drive from Copper Springs, Oregon to Citrus Grove, where we lived. Like he promised, Grandpa was there at ten o'clock sharp. We quickly loaded his truck and jumped in. Daddy hugged Jamaal and fiddled in his hair.

"Hey Pop," he said. "Make sure this boy get a haircut."

Grandpa laughed and opened up his side of the door. "I have to stop in town before we get to Copper Springs. Ponder will cut him up real good."

Daddy lifted up my cap and smiled my smile. He looked at me for a moment as though he was seeing something inside of me that was bigger than my nine year old body frame. "You be good Princess, and no messing around with blue lizards." He winked, and kissed me on the nose, then on the cheek as if he agreed with what me and Jamaal had done to Gretchen, but of course, he would never admit it.

Mama kissed me and Jamaal and handed us both a bag of goodies: fried chicken, a huge tub of watermelon, honeydew, and a bag of brownies, and Snicker doodle cookies for the road. She knew we'd get hungry and that Grandpa had a sweet tooth.

"Act correct," she said," and don't make Papa have to tell you twice." She kissed us again.

"They ain't gonna be no trouble Annette." Grandpa said as he backed out of the driveway. Of course Grandpa didn't say mama's name the way everyone else said it. The A was replaced with an I. Me and Jamaal cracked up every time he said it. Being the boy that he was, Jamaal licked his tongue out at Gretchen who stood in her driveway staring at the both of us with the saddest look on her face.

It was weird. So weird that I couldn't follow Jamaal's lead this time and lick my tongue out at her. I got goose-bumps from her stares on that hot July day. It was as if she didn't want us to go. Grandpa picked up my look. "You okay there," he said.

"Yep," I said. Of course I was lying and I could see that Grandpa could tell.

I didn't like Gretchen. Though I would never tell my mother this, I was sort of proud of how Jamaal and I stuck it to her by putting that blue lizard down her dress. We laughed about it for days. Gretchen swore revenge, but revenge was far from her eyes today. It was a sadness in her eyes that I had never seen; the sort of sadness that comes from one's soul. Oddly enough, it bothered me tremendously. So much so, that I almost asked grandpa to turn around and get her. I couldn't make heads or tails as to why she looked so troubled since she claimed to hate me and Jamaal so much?

However, Jamaal didn't see it, or didn't care. He teased and taunted, and licked his tongue out at Gretchen until her medium frame had vanished from our view. Grandpa's eyes never left me, or the road. He was always overly cautious when he drove us anywhere. But, more than the road, it was me that he was worried about.

"Little girl," Grandpa said, as he stopped at the red light before hitting the freeway. "I don't believe I ever seen you this quiet." He said. "Are you concerned about that little girl back there?" He asked.

"Worried about who?" Jamaal asked, looking at me.

"The girl who you put a blue lizard down her back," Grandpa couldn't help but laugh.

Jamaal turned and faced me and I could tell by the look in his eyes that he was going to come at me long before his words did. I could read his mind like I could read a book.

"Don't be stupid Jazz." He said. Jazz was short for Jasmine. "She insulted you in front of the whole neighborhood. She poked fun at our bikes, pop's truck, and she's always bragging about how much money her parents have." He said. "Don't you be feeling sorry for her, and stop acting like a girl." He tossed his baseball back and forth in his mitt.

Grandpa laughed, but in the same breath, he got at Jamaal. "Hey," he said. "Stop calling your sister stupid, and stop telling her how to feel." He merged into the fast lane. "You hear me."

"Yeah," Jamaal said, embarrassed. "Gretchen hates us. You know she does Jazz."

"She doesn't hate you." He said. "She envies what the two of you have." He switched the truck into another lane. "She wants your life. God bless her heart."

"Her parents are rich Grandpa." I said. "She gets everything she wants."

"Except love," he glanced over at the both of us. "Things cannot replace affection." He said. "You'll see someday."

Grandpa looked in his rearview mirror and took notice of the plastic tub of Snicker doodle cookies. Before he could ask, I opened the tub and put him four big ones in a quart size bag that mama had neatly packed on the inside. I handed Jamaal one, and he took a nice size bite out of the other one. It didn't seem like it, but we had been driving for hours. Cedar Falls was the city outside of Copper Springs and it was huge.

There were banks and restaurants on every corner; high rise buildings that nearly touched the puffy white clouds and Starbucks woven in between quiet corners, and nestled in major grocery stores. It was Oregon alright with clean air that smelled like fresh linens off of a clothesline. Cedar Falls was about twenty five minutes from Copper Springs. It was the place where Grandpa restocked his supplies, bought his groceries, and talked trash to the men at the barber shop about sports and life.

Jamaal and I enjoyed looking at the high rise buildings. The buildings had a unique look and feel, and it was as if the Greek Gods had personally made them. Their Galleria was to die for, and it looked as if Hercules had lived there even though I knew that he didn't. As Grandpa had promised, he took Jamaal to the barbershop and got him a pretty cool haircut. And, I got my cone dipped in chocolate, and my two books, Heidi, and the Three Musketeers. Grandpa filled the truck up with groceries and supplies like candles, fire wood, coil oil, flash lights, and batteries. He got teased some by the city folks about Copper Springs. But, in their teasing, there was a hint of seriousness like they were scared of something out there? Or, more like it, frightened of Girt.

Girt was an old Indian woman; a Cherokee right down to her bones. Copper Springs had been in her family for a Century and two decades. It was rumored that all of her people that had passed on were buried beneath the wild oak trees next to the stables. I never saw evidence of that, and grandpa never mentioned it. But, he did tell Jamaal and I how bankers and developer's constantly made Girt offers, big ones, but Girt always refused to sell. According to Grandpa, this went on for years.

Girt had fought them and fought them hard. And when they saw that they weren't going to win the legal way, well they did things foul. One hot day in July, the banker, developer, and the sheriff showed up at Girts' door and told her she had been ordered to vacate. Town folks said Girt snapped, poisoned the three, and drowned them in the lake by the shed along with herself. Grandpa told another version.

He said Girt summoned her ancestors and all hell broke loose. Copper Springs became a blistering inferno, and everything was destroyed except Girts' shed. Grandpa said that the fire was so bad that the local firemen just had to let it burn out. As far as the two men and the sheriff who showed up that day, it was assumed that they had burned back into the dirt in which they were made. And Girt, it was assumed that she had died to.

But, the mystery of it all was that the shed was untouched, and the water around it bluer than blue. For years no one drove that stretch of road, fear I guess? Grandpa said the rumors drove him nuts, and the curiosity made him crazy. Out of that curiosity, he made the trip out there, after he saw its raw beauty, he knew he had to have it. Copper Springs was practically given to him, and the rest was history.

We pulled into Copper Springs, and as always the smell of pine hit our nostrils like Aunt Zoe's chocolate chip cookies. For miles there was nothing but tall pine trees, and lush green walking trails with all sorts of cool places to roam, hide, and play. In the distance was the barn where Grandpa kept his horses; beautiful mustangs like Passion who was my favorite. She was auburn red with white down the middle. Her hoofs and tail were both white like snow on a cold winter's day.

Her eyes were gentle and caring. When I talked to her, I knew she understood what I was saying. Jamaal swore I was losing my mind. His favorite was a male horse named Boots. His coat was as black as coal, and as shiny as the sun. Odd to say, he had the same characteristics as my brother; cocky, and sure of himself. I'm sure that's why Jamaal was attracted to him.

However, we weren't allowed to ride them if Grandpa or his hand Pulley weren't with us. As we got closer to the house, there was the shed, and the lake where Jamaal and I loved to swim. The shed was creepy. Every time I was near it, the hair on my hair stood on the back of my neck. Something was in there.

I didn't know what. Grandpa swore it was Girt watching out over us and the place. Jamaal of course didn't believe anything at least for now.

As we pulled into Grandpa's circular driveway, the shed opened and closed as if someone came out of it. I jumped and placed my whole body next to Grandpa. Jamaal's eyes widen, but he tried to pretend that he wasn't scared.

"It's my Grandkids Girt." Grandpa said. "This here is Jamaal, My grandson, and this here is my granddaughter Jazzy. They're here with us for a month." He took bags out of the truck.

As if she understood him, the shed opened and closed on its own. Now, I was really spooked. Jamaal tried to act like it wasn't nothing, but I knew he was afraid.

"Just the wind," he said, taking in more groceries and supplies.

"It was not." I followed behind him with bags in my hand.

"Was too," he said. "Scary cat, scary cat, Girt is a myth."

"How would you know if she is? The shed opened and closed by itself. Explain that." I said, and licked out my tongue.

"Nobody's ever seen her Dumbo," he fired back.

"Shut up." I said, and went after him.

"Jamaal, Jazzy, stop that fooling around," Grandpa said. "And stop making faces at each other; don't think I don't see you." He said.

"Gee," Jamaal said, as we entered the kitchen. "Does he have eyes in the back of his head?"

It was weird. He always managed to catch us all the time. Jamaal stood on the step ladder while I pitched him canned goods to put away. We heard Grandpa talking to a strange voice outside the front door. The stranger was middle aged with gray decorating the sides of his hair. The gray seemed to be following some sort of trail in his hair. It had found its way to the middle somehow, making his hair look as if it was skunked. He looked pale and he didn't look like he got much sunlight.

He handed Grandpa his card. Grandpa looked at him and he sort of smiled as if he were familiar with it. "You people just don't quit." He said. "I told your daddy no, and I'm telling you no. This place here is for my grandkids." He said. "Besides," he gave the man back his card. "Even if I did want to sell, Girt doesn't, and as crazy as it may sound, I made her a promise and I don't intend on breaking it."

The man's eyes widened at the mentioning of Girts' name. He must have thought Grandpa was crazy.

"Look EZ," he said to Grandpa. "With the money we're offering you, you can buy your grandkids anything you want and you can take Girt with you." He said.

"Ain't interested," Grandpa said. "Now," he said. "If you'll excuse me, I've got my grandkids to tend to."

When Grandpa returned to the pantry, he had a huge smile on his face as if nothing had ever happened. He seemed pretty amazed that Jamaal and I had gotten the stuff put up so quickly. We asked about the hard chores that mama expected us to do because of what we had done to Gretchen. Grandpa tossed his hand and said, "I'm not thinking about Annette." Jamaal and I cracked at the way he said mama's name.

Grandpa fixed a pot of mashed potatoes and corn to go with the chicken mama had fried for us earlier. For dessert, we finished off the watermelon and honeydew. I had barely enough room to finish my milk. I knew that if I couldn't, Jamaal could.

He had down two glasses already, and the half glass that I had left

would have been cake for him.

"Grandpa," Jamaal said. "Are you going to sale this place?"

"Now what would make you think that," he said.

"We saw the man outside, and we heard what he said."

Jamaal wiped his mouth with a napkin.

"Yeah," I said.

"Only two who will get this place when I'm gone is the two

of you." He said. "I've had this place for over twenty years, and

since things have died down over the years, some of everybody has

been after this place. Copper Springs will always be around for the

both of you to enjoy it."

"Promise," I said.

"Yeah Grandpa, this is the coolest place on earth." Jamaal

said.

"You think so," Grandpa laughed, and we began to clear the

table. My room just happened to be across from the shed.

Sometimes I heard strange noises out there. It sounded like footsteps

walking back and forth. When it spooked me bad, I'd run and

jump in Grandpa's bed. I knew that if I were with him Girt wouldn't bother me.

Sometimes when Jamaal and I swam in the lake, I could feel her eyes watching us from the old crusty window in the shed. I never told Jamaal because I didn't want to be teased, and it would only make him poke around there more.

"Jamaal," I said. "Come on, I wanna go for a swim."

"In a minute," he said. "I think I found something? Hurry before Grandpa sees us." He said.

"No," I said. "I'm not going in there. I'm going swimming." I pulled off my oversized tee shirt.

"Pirates aren't afraid of nothing." He tempted me. He began making chicken sounds. He knew I couldn't stand to be teased, and out of stupidity, I followed him.

"I'm not scared Jamaal." I said. But my knees were shaking so badly and it was hard for me to stand, but I didn't let him know it.

"Look!" He said.

It was a small wooden box that was aged. The corners were chipped, and it was softer than normal wood. There were tiny holes in it. When Jamaal went to open it, the door slammed shut, and a splinter found its way under three layers of skin on my index finger. Jamaal and I both screamed and ran to the door, but it was locked, and I screamed even louder. Jamaal pushed and pulled on the door with all of his twelve year old might, but it didn't budge. And for once, I could see fear all in his face.

"Hey," Grandpa said, as he opened the door with a slight nudge. "What are you kids doing in here?"

I flew into Grandpa's arms crying and shivering like a leaf. I didn't care if we were in trouble. I was just glad that he was there. Grandpa rubbed my back and chuckled hearty. He tossed an arm around Jamaal's shoulder and took us out of the shed.

"Jazzy," he said. Somehow the name Jasmine never quite stuck with him. "Have hog sense girl." He laughed. "Don't be letting this knuckle head talk you into doing things." He put some rubbing alcohol on my finger, squeezed it, burnt the needle, and before I could blink, the splinter was in his hand. "I suppose Girt don't want you all fooling around in her shed."

"I'm not ever going back in there again." I said.

"Well good for you," Grandpa laughed and bandage up my finger.

"It was just the wind." Jamaal said, refusing to admit he was afraid.

"Really," Grandpa said. "Well, you didn't look like it was no wind," he looked over at Jamaal. "Girt scared you near out of your draws." He laughed again.

"Did not," Jamaal frowned.

"Did so," I said.

"If Girt is so real, how come no one's ever seen her?" He said.

"Something made you run like hell out of that shed," Grandpa said. "It ain't what you see in life son, it's what you feel."

Jamaal raised an eyebrow, and he looked at Grandpa weird. By his facial features it was obvious that he was clueless, and at twelve, seeing was everything. Grandpa looked over at the shed as if he were seeing something.

"Girt," he said. "These are my grandkids. They weren't meaning any harm. They're just too curious is all?" He said. "So, I'd appreciate if you wouldn't scare the hell out of them anymore."

The shed settled like an old house. Then, the door opened and closed softly like she had been outside listening to him and had agreed by going in and not slamming the door. I couldn't believe what I was seeing. Neither could Jamaal. For certain, I was not sleeping in my bedroom alone tonight.

"Did you see that?" I said.

"Yeah," he blew me off, and focused on Grandpa. "You actually talk to her?" He asked.

"Yeah, I do, but you don't believe nothing, so it's no point in going any further." Grandpa said.

"I believe you Grandpa." I said. "Girts' in there isn't she?"

"Yeah right," Jamaal fired back.

My finger was a little sore and tender. I didn't want the fresh water to get up under my nail and burn my wound, and I didn't want my gauge to get wet. Jamaal had already jumped into the water and swam around me and Grandpa. He beckoned for me to jump in, but I held up my finger.

"See," he waded in the water. "Told you that you weren't no pirate," he said.

"Am so, but I ain't no fool," I said.

Grandpa laughed and smacked his hands on his thighs. The truth was I yearned to jump into the water and make a big splash on Jamaal, but my finger was hurting, and I didn't want to add to it. I loved swimming. In fact, it was what I lived for at Copper Springs. It was something about the water. The cold thick feel of it on a hot summer day, somehow it soothed my nine year old soul.

Temporarily Girt had ruined that, and so did my dumb brother Jamaal. Me too I guess, for being crazy enough to fall for his taunting. Grandpa wrapped an arm around my shoulder and kissed my cheek. He could always read that look in my eyes like daddy could.

"Come on you two." He said. "If you can't swim, you might as well ride Passion and boots." He helped me up. My complexion changed. Jamaal and I raced each other to the house and quickly changed. By the time Grandpa reached the door, the phone had rung a couple of times. On the last ring, he picked up before it went to voice mail.

"Hey son," he said, taking a seat in the parlor. "The kids are just fine, changing out of their swimming clothes, to riding clothes." He looked over at me and Jamaal. "They," he halted his speech as Jamaal and I waved our hands, signaling that we didn't want to talk.

"They what pop," Dad said.

"Hell I'm old son," Grandpa said, shaking a finger at Jamaal and me. "I'll have them call you after they ride. How's the Caribbean's?" He asked.

"Like paradise," Daddy said. "The water is so clear here that you can see your soul in it."

"And, Annette," he said.

"Let's just say I hope that I can get this woman home in a month." Daddy laughed.

We put our hands over our mouth and giggled at the way he always said mama's name. Jamaal's name was the same. Especially when he pissed Grandpa off, you could hear his Louisiana drawl. It was like when he said Jamaal's name that the "J" was separate. So, Jamaal became Jay mall.

We eased out of the front door closing it very softly. Jamaal took off running and I was in lock step with him in a foot race to the stables where Pulley Harper, Grandpa's friend and hand was waiting on us. Pulley was always glad to see us. He paused from feeding the horses their oats and carrots and made it over to Jamaal and me, and gave us a big old hug.

"Well, well," he smiled. "Look what the cat drug in." Pulley said.

Boots tossed his head back, leaned back with his two front legs raised high in the air, and spoke horse to Jamaal. Jamaal rushed to him and you would have thought a party was going on at the way the two of them carried out. Pulley and I were both use to it. Ask me, the two were made for each other.

My horse was different. Passion was mild and serene. She spoke to me with her eyes, and when I went to her stall, she laid her face next to mines so sweetly. I petted her perfect face. I fed her some carrots, and told her I loved her with each stroke of my hand. Grandpa had finally made it into the stables, and Jamaal and I knew what he was going to say long before he said it.

"You're calling your folks after we're done riding." He said, saddling up passion, while Pulley saddled Boots, then Missy for himself. Grandpa saddled up his favorite sock, who was quite a lot like him. We rode in the front. Pulley and Grandpa were a short distance behind in the back.

This is where you could see the exquisiteness of Copper Springs. And, it was easy to see why developer's wanted it. It was a canvass of beauty. Rolling green hills that uncoiled for miles. Wild pecan and walnut trees out in the middle of nowhere, dropping their treats for the birds and squirrels to eat.

It was like God had dropped a little piece of heaven at Copper Springs just for Grandpa and us to see it. We stopped at the creek to rest our horses and to let them feed on the water. Passion looked as if she were about to drink up the entire creek as thirsty as she was. But slowly her sips came to a crawl, and as quickly as she started, she stopped.

Pulley and Grandpa talked about old people stuff. Jamaal and I searched for four leaf clovers amongst a grass full of dandelions. Whoever found one would make a wish and hold it up to the evening star in hopes that their dream would materialize and come true.

"Look, look," I said. "Jamaal, I found one." I held up my four leaf clover.

"Cool," Jamaal smiled, all excited.

"Grandpa look." I said showing it off to him.

Gonna be blessed girl," he said. "You know how hard it is to find one of those things out here?" He gave me the thumbs up sign.

"Hold it up to the first star." Pulley said. He meant the evening star. "Whatever you wish is gonna come true."

I held it up, closed my eyes, and wished hard. Jamaal was wishing to. I could tell because his hand was on top of mines. I didn't mind. He was my brother, and besides, he nearly guided me to it. He just didn't see it. Boots began to get restless so we headed back, and as we approached the stalls in the barn Jamaal asked me what I wished for.

"You know I can't tell you bubble head." I said. "It won't come true if I do." I pinched him. The kind of pinch you pull, then twist. For that, he chased me to the main house only to see a notice placed on Grandpa's front door.

Before Jamaal and I could start to read it, Grandpa pulled it off the door. The look in his eyes said it all. In fact, they spoke louder than the white piece of paper did. His eyes were tired. His usual joyful demeanor went blank. Jamaal and I stood watching him knowing that something was terribly wrong.

"Go on," he said. "Go you two, wash up for supper." Like typical nine and twelve year olds, we stood like manikins unable to move. Our eyes focused on the letter in Grandpa's hand, and his reaction to it; which I liken it to when Grandma had passed. Grandpa cleared his throat, and looked up at Jamaal and me.

"Didn't I just ask you both to go wash up for supper?" He frowned.

"Yeah, but..." Jamaal said.

"But nothing, go do it then, and don't make me tell you twice."

We knew he was serious when he said that. We opened the wooden screen door, and I paused nearly stepping on Grandpa's shoe.

"Is everything alright Grandpa?" I said. "Are we gonna have to leave here?"

No baby," he folded the letter and placed it in his back pocket. "This place will be yours and Jamaal's one day." He took me by the hand. "God don't bring you to something without a plan to bring you through it." He smiled and kissed my forehead. Instantly I felt better. I don't why, I just did.

Jamaal and I washed our hands and set the table. But, there was wonder in our eyes and in our gut we knew something was horribly wrong. All I could think about was the man in the navy blue suit, how he was inquiring about Copper Springs. It was obvious that he was trying hard to get Grandpa to sell. I could tell by the way Jamaal was looking at me that he was thinking the same thing to.

He was about to say something about it, but the phone rang. He sat the plate down and answered it. It sounded like mama's ring. I don't know how I knew. I just did. I heard him say hello and mama in the same sentence. From a short distance away, I heard Grandpa praying and singing. I couldn't make out what he was saying, but I could feel God in the room. Jamaal pinched my ear, handed me the phone, and finished setting the table.

"It's mama block head. Get your head out of the clouds."
He said.

Before I could say hello, she seemed to sense something was wrong. It always tripped me out when she did that. We were thousands of miles away, and somehow she detected something was out of sorts. What was I supposed to say? Copper Springs is in trouble, and God is in the room? I ended up saying I was hungry. She said; let me speak to your Grandpa.

The timing could not have been more perfect. Grandpa came out of his room humming. As he did, the shed opened wide, and then closed again all by itself. I did a double take, wiped my eyes, but I knew what I had saw. Grandpa took the phone from me. He signaled for me to put the bread he had made earlier into the bread basket and I did.

I heard Grandpa ask mama about the Caribbean's and then I heard him laugh his hearty laugh, and that was it. Jamaal had tapped my shoulder so much that he had made it sore. He was trying to get my attention about the shed. It had opened again apparently and it had gotten his attention.

"Did you see that?" He said.

"See what?" I said.

"The shed, it opened just now. You didn't see that," he looked scared.

"No," I said. "Earlier I did."

"When?" He asked.

Before I could answer, Grandpa had handed me the phone first to say goodbye to mama, then Jamaal. By the time we had hung up with mama, I had forgotten what Jamaal had asked. Grandpa prayed over the meal: pot roast, homemade bread, peach cobbler, and sweet tea. All during dinner, Grandpa didn't mention anything about what was on that white piece of paper. His eyes were serene, and his demeanor unflustered, but the shed was restless.

Three days later my finger had healed from the splinter that had found its way under a couple of inches of my skin. It was as good as new, not even a bruise, or a scar. This was my favorite thing to do at Copper Springs was to swim; swim until I was tired, leaving just enough energy to get out of the water and lay in my chair for hours letting the sun dry my wet skin.

Jamaal and I were having so much fun that neither of us paid attention to the restlessness of the shed. We were too busy splashing each other and having water fights.

Suddenly, everything changed. The wind rose and the doors of the shed kept opening and closing rapidly. The sunlight faded, and all of a sudden it was pitch black outside. Grandpa appeared out of nowhere, and pulled both Jamaal and I out of the water.

"Come on," he said, rushing us.

I don't know what made me look back but I did. The lake water was bubbling like it was hot, and there was a hooded figure in the shed window. Jamaal saw it to, and he screamed; so unlike him. I screamed to. We made it to the front porch shaken, scared. If Grandpa would not have held unto me so tight, I swear I would have fainted.

This was not the Copper Springs that we knew. There were rumors yes, all kinds, but this was real, and I was scared to death. The man in the dark navy suit that had spoken to Grandpa days ago had driven up in the driveway along with the Sheriff.

"Go," Grandpa said, but we refused.

"We tried to be reasonable Ezekiel. We made you a generous offer for this place, but you refused." The man in the dark suit said. "I'm afraid I'm not as patient as my father." He said, and then a tree fell on his car and destroyed it.

His eyes widen, and even from where I stood, I could see fear in them, and he hid behind the Sheriff. The Sheriff placed his hand on his gun. His eyes were terrified, and he knew he was fighting against something he couldn't shoot.

"I don't know what the hell is going on here Ez." The Sheriff said. "But..."

"Get out of here before somebody gets hurt. Girt ain't gonna give up this land." Grandpa said.

"Give Girt this then," The Sheriff attempted to hand Grandpa a notice, but something snatched it out of his hand.

Before we could blink, old Girt appeared right in front of the sheriff. I'll never forget what she looked like. She was medium height with two long black braids that touched the lower part of her back. She wore a gray cloak with a hood attached. Jamaal and I saw Girt from the back mind you so, I hadn't a clue of what her face looked like.

She looked at the paper and blew on it. Instantly, it became ashes. The Sheriff's and the man in the dark suit eyes lit up like a Christmas trees, and they practically ran over each other getting into the Sheriff's car. However, Girt wasn't done. As they attempted to back out of Grandpa's driveway, Girt made a circle with her finger. The Sheriff backed right into it, and like magic, the car disappeared and so did the circle.

I screamed, and then Jamaal screamed. Grandpa comforted us and calmed us down. My legs knocked like an aging old man. It was weird, I felt as though my life had been snatched out of me. Temporarily my body was a shivering shell; that was until Girt turned and looked at Grandpa, and I saw her eyes. They were gentle, and lonely, but I could tell she trusted my Grandpa, and her spirit had willed him her land.

Jamaal was still stuck to Grandpa like a stamp to a letter. His eyes told me what his mouth couldn't, that he was petrified. And, it was most interesting and unfortunate how he learned to believe in things he couldn't see. From that point on, life was different for Jamaal and me too. Nobody ever bothered Grandpa again about Copper Springs. Things quietly went back to normal. Jamaal and I went back to riding horses, swimming, and we felt Girt watching us.

On occasion, I would see a shadow lurking by the window, but I felt safe. I felt like putting blue lizard's down Gretchen's back was worth it, without it, Copper Springs would not have been saved. We grew a lot that summer; not in inches, but in faith. It wasn't a big deal anymore to us that Gretchen was rich and we weren't. Yeah, she could have anything she wanted, but she didn't have what Jamaal and I had.

Jamaal was my brother and I'll admit he did get on my invisible nerve at times. But I loved him. He taught me a lot. We did have the time of our lives that summer, and we've never stopped talking about it even until this day. For years I had kept what I wished for a secret. Jamaal wanted to know after all these years. I sort of figured it was cool to tell it. Plain and simple, I wished for Copper Springs to be saved and it was. Gretchen might have had the French Rivera that year, but we had Copper Springs, Grandpa, and Girt and we grew in places that she never would.

The end

# Love Will Find A Way

Deja looked endlessly for her journal. She looked through packed boxes, bins, and even her luggage. She looked everywhere. And out of thin air, it seemed to have vanished. She was frustrated and she didn't know what to make of it.

"Mom," she yelled from her bedroom.

"Yeah baby," her mother said.

"Have you seen my pink journal?" She sat on her bed exhausted from looking. "You know the pink one that said *"dream"* on it." She said.

Marissa dried her hands on a dry dish cloth, and walked down the hall to her daughter's room. She stood in the entry way, arms folded across her chest, smiling at her discouraged daughter as if she knew something wonderful.

"No, I haven't. But what you love honey you never lose." She said.

"Well mama, I've lost my journal. Daddy bought me that journal." She sighed in frustration as she looked at her mother. "It was the last thing he gave me." Her eyes watered a little.

Marissa took a seat next to her daughter and took her into her arms, kissing her forehead. "It'll show up, I promise; in a place that you least expect."

"Well, I hope so because all of my dreams are in there." Deja said.

"No," her mother lifted her face and held it so delicately in her hands. "All of your secrets are in there. Your dreams are in here." She placed her hand over her heart. "Now, let me see a smile on that pretty face of yours," she kissed her forehead again. "I've made your favorite for lunch." She took her by the hand and guided her to the kitchen.

Immediately, Deja's sorrows were lifted once she saw a plate of fried green tomatoes, French fries; a pitcher of Sweet Tea, and a homemade peach pie taken right from the oven. She blessed the food and placed slices of fried tomatoes on wheat bread and ate. Her mother's cooking was like a warm hug. Eating it was comforting, and finishing off a glass of her Sweet Tea was healing.

"See," Deja said. "This is what I am going to miss. I can't make food taste like this and do this." She ate more fries.

Girl please," her mother said. "Only thing this food does is quiet that hungry belly of yours."

"No," Deja shook her head with food in her mouth. "Mama, you don't get it. Your food heals. It truly is comfort food. You see," she placed her plate in the kitchen sink. "I'm not even upset anymore."

"Well good," her mother said, and bit into her tomato sandwich.

"Mama," Deja cut a slice of pie and placed it on her plate. "Come with me. I don't like the fact of you being here alone."

"Baby I love this house. Your father and I raised all five of our children here, including you." She paused from eating. "My friends are here. Your aunt Summer is here. My church is here." She wiped her mouth and poured herself another glass of Sweet Tea. "Besides, I think Barney our mailman would be pretty pissed if his ham sandwich and lemonade wasn't sitting on the porch waiting for him." She paused again before she drunk. "After all, he's been getting that sandwich and lemonade from me for thirty-seven years."

Deja looked at her mother and smiled. What else was she supposed to do? It was who her mother was. Who she had always been, and she could see why her father Hezekiah had fallen in love with her. If only she could be so fortunate to find that type of love?

She didn't dare tell her mother, but she had given up on love. After her sister Zeya had gotten married three years ago this past June, and given birth three months ago to a baby girl; that had told her all what she needed to know. Maybe it was time that she settled into being a great aunt; being the one buying the expensive gifts like taking little Deja to Disney World. Despite how she felt, she still wondered how her mother and Zeya had gotten so lucky.

"You go live your life. And all that you've ever hoped for will find you." She kissed her cheek. "I promise to come visit once you get settled in. You know I'm a text away."

Deja was tired. She had unpacked all but two boxes. Hopefully her journal would show up in one of them. At any case, she would go through the remaining boxes tomorrow. She tried to fight her sleep, but exhaustion had over taken her. In a deep, restful sleep, she dreamt her journal had been given to her as a gift by a strange man with a beautiful smile that could lite up a room.

As the strangers face became clearer, a soft tap at her door penetrated her ears, and gently woke her up. She stretched, paused a second. But, the tapping persisted as if it were drawing her to the door. An odd look overshadowed her face, cautiously she went to the door, and peeped out of the peep hole. Suddenly the tapping stopped, and the handsome gentlemen began to walk away with a smile on his face. She had seen that smile before, and it was his smile that made her open her door.

"Excuse me," she called out to him.

He turned and walked back to her door. The same smile that had gotten her to open the door stood boldly on his face. He cleared his throat, but his smile persisted.

"I saw the mover's, and I just thought that I'd bring you some lasagna, a chocolate cake, and a bottle of Zinfandel. I bought it just up the road at a retreat in Napa." He said. "I know what it's like to move. Things are all over the place, and I just wanted to welcome you to the neighborhood."

"Wow!" Deja said. "This is awfully sweet of you. I was down the hall trying to put things away." She lied.

"Don't explain." He said. "Like I said, I know what it means to move."

"Please come in." Deja said.

He entered and sat her meal and her wine on her dining room table. Denarius was pretty amazed at what she had gotten done. There were pictures, paintings, and murals on her walls. Vertical blinds and valances hung beautifully throughout. When he had first moved in his home a few years back, his place looked like a tornado had hit it. How did she do it?

"Looks good already," he said, looking around. "By the way, I'm Denarius Allen, and I'm your neighbor across the street." He extended his hand.

"I'm Deja Corey." She shook his hand. "Would you like to stay and help me eat some of this lasagna? It's pretty big for one person." She began taking down some dinnerware her mother had bought her.

"I..," he was interrupted by his smart phone. "Now," he said. "I'm on my way." He sighed and flashed that smile again. "It seems that I'm going to have to take a rain check on lunch.

I've just been summoned by the hospital, so enjoy the food and the wine." He said and rushed out the door.

The lasagna was still hot and it smelled delicious. The cake looked amazing; a lucky guess by a stranger that he fathomed chocolate cake was her favorite. Her Samsung phone sung to her. By the song it sang, "I Just Called to Say I Love You," she knew it was her mother.

Her mother had left her a text. "I'm sure you're busy unpacking. I just wanted to say that I love you and next weekend I'm driving down to see you. Call me later. Oh and by the way, your journal's going to show up soon if it already hasn't. Love you much."

Deja smiled at her mother's text. She tasted the lasagna and it wooed her mouth, and excited her hungry stomach. If the lasagna was this good, she couldn't wait to taste the chocolate cake. What kind of neighborhood was this that handsome men knocked on your door and brought food and wine? She poured herself a glass of wine and finished off her lasagna.

She sat her dish in the sink and took down a saucer from her cabinet. She stared at the cake briefly as if she could resist it, but she couldn't. As she cut the cake, Denarius allowed the new father to cut the umbilical cord of his baby boy. He had seen that smile a million times and each time he saw it, he knew that he had chosen the right profession. He smacked the new father on the shoulder with a smile.

"You did good man." He said, making his way to the proud mother.

"Sorry, I messed up your shirt." She said.

"Ah don't worry about it," he placed her hand in his. "I've got a dozen of these things. I'm proud of you mom you did it." He patted her hand. "You got the little fellow here. We're gonna keep you and him a few days or so to make sure things are alright, then you can go." He said. "I'll check on you both tomorrow to see how things are progressing." He left the delivery room.

As he entered his office, he removed the soiled shirt, and showered. Now he understood why the Chief of Staff was so insistent on all the OBGYN's having shower's in their offices.

For this same reason, he left a couple of clean shirts and pants in his office closet. He was supposed to be on vacation, but babies of course could care less. He made a few phone calls, checked his calendar, and left. It was his favorite aunt Candice's birthday and he knew just what she wanted, and just where he would get it.

It was a beautiful fall day in Seaside, California. The Valley Oaks had begun to turn yellows, rust, and auburn. All along the roadside, Valley Oaks, Blue Oaks, and wild fig trees lined the curb. Denarius always took the side roads during that time of the season just so he could look at the fall foliage. It was soothing and during hectic times at the hospital he would drive down them just to relax.

He pulled up to the Pathway, a vintage stationary store that was as old as Seaside. He waived to the owner's and made his way into the shop. The smell of Sweet Potato Pie hit him as he entered the door. He loved the smell. It reminded him of his mother's Sweet Potato Pie, and every time he smelled it he wanted to rush Thanksgiving.

Dorothy and her sister Amelia had run the store for years. They had aged modestly, but their store had not. They were kind and sweet old ladies and they always greeted him with warm hugs.

"Well, look what the cat done drug in." Dorothy said.

"How you been sweet pea?" Amelia patted his cheek.

"Good, good," he said.

"How's practice," Dorothy asked.

"I'm blessed Mrs. Dorothy, in fact, I just delivered an anxious one today." He laughed.

"Aren't you supposed to be on vacation?" Amelia stacked shelves with new books with Deja's book being placed on the front shelf. But Denarius hadn't noticed.

"Like what that got to do with it girl, when those babies get anxious to see the world, they're coming." Dorothy laughed, putting journals on the back shelf that had just arrived.

"I hear you Mrs. Dorothy." He browsed.

"I guess you right girl." Amelia said. "I was just thinking that maybe if he sat still long enough, he'd find a nice girl and settled down.

"I feel you." Dorothy said. "And deliver his own baby, you got a sweetie?"

"No ma'am, Mrs. Right has not showed up yet," he continued to look. Suddenly, he found what he was looking for. A red, soft leather bound journal with a blue butterfly in the center. The size was perfect. He knew she would love it. Red was his aunt's favorite color and butterflies decorated her office.

He hadn't seen a woman who loved butterflies so much. They decorated the top and bottom of her weekly column. Sometimes he wondered if she were a butterfly in her past life. He made his way to the counter. Dorothy stopped what she was doing and came to the front.

"Found what you were looking for baby?" She said.

"Yeah, yeah, I think so?" He looked at the wording around the butterfly. *"Love Will Find Away."*

"That's beautiful baby, your aunt is going to love it." She rang it up.

The journal Denarius purchased jolted Dorothy's memory and she remembered the box that came with their regular shipment. It was mysterious alright; strange to say the least. It was as if the box was meant to come there.

Its only identification was the initials of DC. At any case they wanted Denarius to give it to his Aunt Candice as a birthday gift.

Dorothy and Amelia set up a display case for folks that had moved, or forgotten they had packages somewhere. Pathway produced lots of foot traffic. There were times when people would come in, see their items and claim them. This was done to return items to their rightful owners. However, the journal that was in the box captured her attention. One because it was pink, the other because it had different colors of blue on the front of it that said *"Dream."*

"Wait," she said to Denarius. "I have something for that Aunt of yours."

She went to the back and returned with the journal. "Here," she gave it to him. "It was odd wasn't it Amelia." Dorothy looked toward her sister.

"Yeah child, you talking about that box that came with our shipments. Give him that journal for Candice. I'm sure she'd love it. Don't look like it's ever been used."

"I just did." Dorothy said.

"It's our gift to her; well one gift anyway." Amelia said.

"Thanks," he smiled. "I'll make sure she gets it." He looked at it. "Well ladies, I have to go, but as always, it's been a pleasure. Have a blessed day."

Where had the day gone? Just this morning, he was making lasagna and chocolate cake for his new neighbor. And before he could share a meal with her, he was paged by the hospital to deliver a baby.

Evening had set in and Denarius had hoped to unwind. He opened a fresh bottle of Riesling poured himself a glass and took a sip. He looked at the journal he had bought his aunt and he smiled. He knew she would love it. He flipped through it noticing that each page had a different color and a different color butterfly at the top and bottom of each page.

He took another sip of wine, and placed the journal in the gift box and set it on his shelf. Then, he pulled out the journal that Dorothy and Amelia had given him for his aunt Candice. Past the pink, it was a nice journal. He set his wine glass on the table, and propped his feet on his ottoman and studied the journal more.

Unlike the journal he had bought his aunt, this one snapped on the side. He was curious. Was dream placed on every page like the butterflies in his aunt's journal? He had to find out and when he unsnapped it, he was stunned.

It was someone's journal. And, it had been written in daily until the last page was full. He flipped through it but there was no forwarding address, or name of the person in which he could send it to. The only clue of who had written in it was the initials DC. He sighed and sipped more of his wine. What was he to do?

How would he find the author of the journal? He thought for a second, and then picked the journal up again. And as if something was egging him on, he surprised himself and began reading it at the same time she was thinking it.

"I've known you before we were born. We just haven't met yet. However, God did say that there is a time and place for all things. And, there is a time for the both of us to meet. I'm unsure how we will meet. Something inside tells me that you won't be a second late. Destiny has already penciled you in and the timing will be perfect." Deja paused in thinking. Denarius paused from reading.

He was impressed with the author's confidence, and the passion woven within each word. He tried to put it down, but he couldn't. She tried to dismiss the importance of finding her journal, but she couldn't. She had one box left to unpack and the thought of it not being there terrified her.

Her phone rung twice, and on the third ring she answered it. The caller ID on her land line gave way to high profile columnist Candice Collins who could touch a book and thrust it to best seller status. Surprised, Deja spoke. "Hello."

"This is Candice Collins, and I certainly hope that I have the pleasure of speaking with my favorite author, Deja Corey."

"Speaking," she said, with a stint of surprise still dangling in her voice.

"I read your new book, Love Will Find A Way, and I could not put it down." Candice said.

"Thank you." Deja was stunned by her words. Candice had a reputation. As quick as she could make you, she could break you with a stroke of her keyboard. She was picky, blunt and at times down right judgmental.

But when she loved a novel, she could thrust a career into a phenomenon no one had ever seen. *"Love Will Find A Way"* was Deja's fourth book; nervous, Deja blurted out thank you again.

"No beloved, thank you." She said. "Where have you been all of my life? And how in the hell did you write such an incredible book?" She seasoned her coffee. "I called that agent of yours, and damn near threatened her for your number." She snickered.

"After reading that book of yours, I was not about to let her off the phone until she gave it to me." She sipped her coffee, and added another spoonful of sugar.

"We must talk beloved. My mind is made up, and I have decided to share you and this blessed novel of yours with the world in my next column." She tasted her coffee again this time it was perfect.

"I don't know what to say." Deja was still trying to recover from the comments Candice had made regarding her book.

"Just say that you'll meet me for lunch tomorrow at one o'clock. I know this perfect ocean front bistro with the best seafood you'll ever eat. You do like seafood don't you beloved?" She asked.

"I love it." Deja said.

"Perfect. Oh, welcome to Seaside. I hear you've just relocated here." She said.

"Yeah," Deja decided to sit before she fell down over Candice's reaction over her book.

"Beloved," she said. "It's very easy to find. I'm sending you the directions via my smart phone to yours. You should get it any minute now." She said. "If you have any problems getting here, don't hesitate to call my cell. It'll be at the bottom of the text."

"Sure," Deja said.

"Anytime, and thank you so much for your time beloved. I look forward to meeting with you and talking to you about that wonderful book of yours. See you at one o'clock sharp." She said and hung up.

Deja was floored. She tried to scream but nothing came out. Instead her heart thumped like a bass drum. Her body shivered like she was having a chill. Her Samsung phone hummed and sung at the same time. One was a text message with directions from Candice. The other was a call from her mother.

"Hello," she said, wiping tears from her eyes.

"Baby," her mother said. "You okay?"

"I am great mama. Candice Collins just called me. She's previewing my book in her column. She said she loved it." Deja got excited.

"What!" Her mother said.

"Yeah," Deja wiped away happy tears. "She's invited me to lunch and she's interviewing me tomorrow."

"Are you serious?" Her mother was stunned.

"Yes, I can't believe it." She said.

"Well I can, my daughter just happens to be a great writer. And apparently I am not the only one who thinks so." Her mother said.

"I can't believe this is happening." Deja said.

"It's the lord baby. He's found favor and it's your turn."

"I'll say it is." Deja said. "I don't think that I am going to be able to sleep a wink tonight."

Her words seem to bode well for Denarius. He couldn't sleep either. The journal was like a good novel. It was a page turner.

With each page he turned, he felt his heart feel things that he never knew he was capable of feeling. At the end of DC's journal, he had fallen in love, and he wrecked his brains on how he would find her.

Denarius slept so soundly that he didn't hear his aunt Candice leave a message for him on the phone. What awakened him was his neighbor's dog Blitz. Blitz had turned over his trashcan. It startled him in his sleep and he immediately hopped up.

He glossed over his face with his hand, and stood looking out his bedroom window. Blitz saw him and took off with a left over piece of steak that he had in his mouth. "Damn Dog," Denarius yawned.

He yawned again and shook off the sleepy, and took notice of his wall clock that read a quarter past eleven. Suddenly his mind went into fast forward, and he remembered that he was supposed to meet his aunt Candice for lunch at noon. The red button flashed constantly on his phone. He knew it was his aunt Candice long before he listened to the message.

He called her on her cell immediately and she answered. "How's my favorite nephew doing?" She asked.

"I'm blessed." He said. "I can't complain. Listen, I'm sorry I missed your call. It's…"

"Those baby's, I know. There so excited to see this world." She gathered her things. "I'll make dinner." She said. "Maybe, I'll get the surprise of my life and hear that my nephew has a good woman in his life."

"Well," he thought about DC's journal, if he were ever fortunate enough to find her. He would be introducing his aunt and his parents to DC.

"Well what?" Candice paused.

"Well, who's this person your meeting at the bistro that's got you so excited?" He said.

"She is the best author I've read in years; gives me goose bumps. Her new book, Love Will Find A Way, was magnificent. I tell you sweet pea this woman is brilliant.

"Really," he smiled.

"Yes, really," she tossed her bag on her shoulder. "Deja Corey is…"

"Did you say Deja Corey?" He said.

"Yes, why, or haven't you been listening." She said.

"If it's the Deja Corey I'm thinking about, she's my new neighbor." He said.

"What!" Candice dropped her keys on her marble floor. "And just when were you going to tell me this?"

"I didn't know she was a writer, and I certainly didn't know that you were going to discover her book." He yawned.

"Sweet pea, you've got to be more conscious of these things. I had to go through a lot to track this woman down, only to discover that she's the new neighbor of my nephew." She sighed, and picked up her keys. "Sweet pea, I've got to go I'm meeting her in twenty minutes. See you for dinner later. Love you."

"Love you to," he hung up.

Denarius experienced a delayed reaction of being shocked. He didn't know what to think. His thoughts raced, and immediately he picked up the journal from his shelf and opened it. There was the signature DC, bold, thick and pronounced. But, it didn't prove anything.

Anyone could have those initials; anyone could have written in a journal and misplaced it.

However, none of this made sense. The Journal was given to him at a stationary store. How it had arrived there was a complete mystery.

He had planned on giving it to his aunt, but then by accident he discovered it belonged to someone. Out of curiosity, he began to read it, and in love, he couldn't put it down. He connected to the author of this journal and she was everything that he had ever wanted in a woman but never thought he would find.

He had sworn to God and himself that he would search the entire earth for this woman. Since reading the journal, he thought about her day and night. There was no way that DC and Deja Corey could be the same person; no way was the universe that kind.

Late afternoon, had brought a subtle chill to the Seaside air. Deja was on a high from her lunch with Candice Collins, and between her mother and her agent, she rattled on, and on about it. Love Will Find A Way had popped into her head at her sister's wedding. Her sister, the budding bride had found the one. Anyone watching the two of them could tell.

The same day after she had come home, she relented to her room. She felt compelled to write in her *"dream"* journal. It sat on her shelf for years waiting for her soul to open up, and it seemed right to record her dreams in it so she did. This time she decided to write God a letter and tell him about the man she wanted, and hoped like her sister Zeya would find him one day.

Her sister's wedding day had come and gone. Out of impatience, and frustration she had given up hope. But, because her father had given her that journal, and she had poured her soul out to God, she wanted her journal back. She was unpacking her last box with the hope that it would be there, but it wasn't, just as she had thought. Her day had been great and she didn't want the journal to sour her mood.

"God please, please give me back my journal." She blinked away the tears. "I know I said that if I ever misplaced it somehow that I'd want my soul mate to find it, and read it so he'd know how to find me. Well, just forget about that; just bring it back to me safely please." Deja pleaded.

The doorbell rang. Deja quickly wiped her tears, rose from her knees, and looked through the peep hole, then opened the door. "Hi," she looked surprised to see Denarius.

"Hi," he said.

"Come on in." She closed the door behind him. She quickly wiped her cheeks again making sure it didn't look like she had been crying.

"I'm sorry." He said. "We're you in the middle of something? He looked at the box of unpacked items on the floor.

"Nothing important," she said, "just looking for something."

"Well," he smiled. "I've got a gift for you." He handed her a pink gift box with a beautiful white bow on top.

She looked surprised, and said. "Thank you, but you really didn't have to."

"I know I didn't. But, I really think you're going to love it." He said. "Open it."

"Okay, okay if you insist." She opened the box and uncovered the pink tissue paper. There it was, her journal and she screamed. "Oh my God! Oh my God!" She looked at Denarius and she knew.

The End

## *Brother's From Different Mother's*

They were meant to be brother's; not by blood, but by spirit. Before they were born, they were destined to find each other. For their sakes, destiny would become today; August 3, 2009, at the bus station in Fremont, Oregon.

Jacob lit up a cigarette and breathed diseased smoke into the still Oregon air. A hundred things roamed through his brain: What was he doing there? How did his life get so jacked up? He shook his head, took another puff of his cigarette and released the filthy smoke again into the clean air. He felt like giving up, and his duffle bag showed it. It was huge, gray and heavy. And, he carried all that he owned in it. In the front, the writing was bold, thick, and white. It said, "Screw You." And, that's pretty much how he felt.

"Hey," said the old man, dressed in a perfectly pressed security uniform.

"Talking to me?" Jacob said, looking directly into the sea blue eyes of the old man. Jacob's accent was thick. He was born in Tulun, Russia a small timber and mining town where the people were a hard working poor.

At the age of ten he was adopted by an American family who just wanted a son to love.  But, his anger ran deep from a secret that only he knew, and because of it, he didn't know how to return the love that his parents had for him.

"Don't see nobody else smoking except you," he said.

"So," Jacob said.

"So, put it out.  Don't you see the sign, or can't you read boy?"  The old man said

He looked up at the sign that was directly up in front of him, only he hadn't noticed it:

Smoking is prohibited in the state of Oregon in public places under Oregon state law, subject to penal code 917638294; violator's will be fined $ 500.

"Ah hell," he said.  "Didn't see it," he took one last draw from his cigarette and put it out.  The old man walked away and rolled his eyes.  Jacob cursed underneath his breath, and while he aired out his frustrations, a blue and white bus pulled up.  When the double doors opened, two young men around seventeen, his age, exited the bus.

Ezekiel had neat, tight, curly black hair like that of a Raven. His skin was chocolate and his right arm had a tattoo of a rosary on it. He had an Mp3 player with ear plugs in both ears, and the book, "Rain Maker," in his hand. By the position of the book marker in his book, it was obvious that he had read over half of it. He too had a duffle bag over his shoulder. And like Jacob's, his bag reflected how he felt. It said, "Whatever!"

Behind Ezekiel, was Caleb. Caleb wore glasses that hid his maple brown eyes. He had an Oakland A's baseball cap on his head. And, he also had a matching baseball shirt that matched his cap. Like Ezekiel, he had an Mp3 player with one ear plug in his ear. Across his golden brown skin, was a duffle bag that said, "Bring It!"

"Anybody sitting here?" Ezekiel and Caleb said in unison. They looked at each other and smiled briefly.

"No, no," Jacob said in shock to see two guys around his same age.

Up until they had gotten off the bus, all he had seen were old people walking gingerly with tiredness in their eyes. Jacob cleared his throat; looked at Caleb and Ezekiel. Before he could plan what he was going to say, it just came out like he was supposed to say it. "Where are you headed?" Jacob asked.

"Me," Caleb looked, almost surprised that Jacob was talking to him.

"Yeah," Jacob snickered.

Caleb took the paper from his back pocket. Just as he was about to say where he was going, a red minivan pulled up.

"Porter Ranch," Floyd said in a soothing voice. "Porter Ranch."

Caleb stood, put the paper back in his pocket as he heard Floyd call out Porter Ranch again. He gathered his things, and looked at Jacob and boarded the van.

"Me too," Jacob grabbed his things.

"Good day gentlemen." Floyd said.

"Hey," Caleb said, taking a seat behind Floyd.

Jacob of course said nothing and took a seat across from Caleb on the right hand side. The seats were comfortable and soft.

It felt like his body was supposed to be sitting there at that very moment, in an odd sense, it felt weird.

"Is he with you all?" Floyd asked, looking at Ezekiel.

"Don't know him," Jacob said.

Ezekiel had pulled one plug out of his ear. He looked at his watch as if he were waiting for someone.

"Young man," Floyd called out to him. "Headed to Porter Ranch?"

"Yeah, yeah," he began gathering his things.

"Lucky it wasn't no snake boy," the old man shook his head. "Cause if it were, it would have bit you right good. Young people," he shook his head.

"Whatever man," Ezekiel said, and boarded the van.

"You spend your whole life looking for something that ends up being right in front of you." The old man said, standing in front of the van.

Floyd laughed. He knew the old man. In fact, he knew Samuel all too well. He rented a room out to him on the ranch after his wife Lily passed away.

He and a few ranch hands attended to the produce farm. He was a bit cranky, but he never let him down, and he could always depend on him.

"Gotta hand it to you Floyd, you know how to pick'em." He said.

"I think you have it wrong Sam. I believe that the good lord led them to me." Floyd smiled.

"If you say so," Sam frowned.

He looked at the three boys the way he had looked at all the rest of them; hard heads who thought they knew everything and knew nothing. Porter Ranch had so much potential. Why was Floyd wasting his time on young punks who had given up on themselves a long time ago? He waved good-bye and walked away.

Floyd looked at all the three boys in his rearview mirror. Jacob pretended to be the tough guy, but beneath the layer's he could see that he was scared. Ezekiel didn't care about anything; which was why he kept his plugs in his ears listening to music. It was how he drowned out life. Caleb wanted to change, but he didn't know how.

Floyd could see a hint of hope in his eyes no matter how he tried to hide it.

Caleb leaned back in his seat, and closed his eyes. Like Jacob, he felt a sense of comfort, and in a strange sense, he felt that where he was headed was where he belonged. But, it couldn't be. Caleb was only seventeen, and thus far in his crazy life, he hadn't belonged anywhere.

Ezekiel, who sat directly in back of Jacob, had fallen to sleep. His head lay slouched over; his mouth opened, and his ear plugs very much in his ears. Floyd couldn't help but smile when he saw Ezekiel sleeping. It was the way old men slept; done with the hardships of life; having overcome the troubles of youth that had taken them from boys to men. If he lived to be an old man who learned to struggle with his demon's and overcame, he would earn that sleep, and when he would wake up, he'd be at peace. Ezekiel yawned and gradually woke up from a deep sleep, but he was still tired.

The beauty of Porter Ranch was stunning. Wild pecan tree's stood in front of white picket fences where horses ran free.

The boy's eyes said all what their mouths couldn't. As they drove down a long stretch of beauty, they watched men harvest vegetables and fruits. They saw patches of wild flowers scattered in the distance in patterns around an old but stable oak tree.

"This is my place." Floyd smiled. "Like it?" He said, pulling up to the main house; waving to his wife Sapphire.

"This is all yours?" Ezekiel said. "This place is off the charts man." Ezekiel had finally uttered more than two words.

Floyd laughed as he got out of the van. "So, the dead has come to life."

"I'm just saying." Ezekiel said, pulling back the van door.

"Damn!" Jacob said.

"Young man," Sapphire came out to meet the boys as she always had. "I don't allow no cursing, nor swearing in my house, or on this place. You understand?" She looked at all of them.

"Yes ma'am," Jacob said, and the other two echoed behind him.

"Breakfast is at 7:30am, lunch is at 12:30pm, and dinner at 5:30pm, don't be late."

They stood quiet, starry-eyed not knowing what to say. Floyd kissed his wife, smiling at her tenderly the way he had smiled at her the first day he met her some fifty years ago at the naval base where she was a nurse. Sapphire turned and walked away smiling looking over her shoulder like a dizzy school girl.

The boys laughed and snickered at the tender moment between Floyd and his wife more than immature giggling, it was a nervous laughter. From the families they had come from, neither of them ever witnessed their parents or parent showing any sort of affection towards them, or their father's if they knew them.

The guesthouse the boys were to stay in was a very short distance away from the main house. The house sat on a parcel by the lake that connected to a dock with a small boat. Floyd and Samuel often used the boat to fish, and sometimes just to relax on lazy summer days. Jacob came to a standstill as he eyed the boat at the dock.

For miles, there was nothing but blue. He wondered if beyond the water if there were land on the other side? Floyd paused at the door, looking over his shoulder. Without thinking about it, he knew exactly what Jacob was thinking.

"Nobody's ever made it out of here on that boat out there." He placed the key in the door. "By six o'clock it's pitch black out there. If by chance the boat picks up a current and starts a slow sail towards Washington State, the fidgety currents will turn the boat over." He looked directly at Jacob. "And if by chance it doesn't, and you head into the Canadian border, you'll freeze to death." He turned the key. "And, if the cold don't kill you, the sharks will." He opened the door.

Ezekiel and Caleb snickered as they entered the guesthouse. Jacob however just rolled his eyes. Who said he was thinking about leaving there? Cherry wood floors welcomed them inside the three bedroom house. A huge circular rug lay in the middle of the floor. A coffee table with a large print bible sat on the table comfortably waiting.

There was a mural of an old mill that covered the entire wall. A beautiful sunset poured over the peak of the mountains. It gave the living room a sense of peace. They followed Floyd to the family room where a huge, big screen television, couch recliners, love seat, and lazy boy chair with an ottoman graced the family room.

Behind them was a modest kitchen; from the kitchen was a sliding glass door that led to a comfortable backyard with a patio and view of the lake.

Floyd brought them back in and showed them their rooms. He then handed each young man a set of keys. Their eyes lit up like Christmas tree's as they were handed keys. No one had trusted them with anything, especially keys. Keys to them were like forbidden fruit and they were the doorway to trouble. So why was Floyd giving them keys? Could this be a set up? They didn't let Floyd know it, but they were all scared; even Jacob a little.

Floyd and the boys migrated back to the living room. Floyd stood in the middle, and they stood in front of him. "I've read all your files and I know your crimes." He said, folding his arms across his chest. "Looks like to me that the good lord is giving you all a second chance," he looked at all of them. "I'd make the very best of it if I were you. Sometimes good breaks get tired of following around folks who disrespect their favor." He sighed. "Oh, another thing, there's no smoking on any part of this property period."

"None," Jacob's eyes widen.

"None," he said. "You smoke?"

"Well yeah," he said. "I paid seven bucks for my smokes."

"So, I'm just supposed to get rid of my smokes?" Jacob's tone changed.

"Either that, or go into the state of Washington to smoke them. This is a smoke free state son."

Jacob's face turned red. This took him back to the old man at the bus stop and the signage just above him. For the life of him, he couldn't understand why people in Oregon freaked out so much over cigarettes? Judging from Sam, the people in Freemont were old and bothered with an agenda against people who were different. It was obvious this wasn't the place for him. He would call his parole officer in the morning and ask to be reassigned.

"Also," Floyd said. "No drinking, wild parties, or girls. Curfew is 9pm, lights out at 9:30pm." He cleared his throat. "Oh, take a look around. This place is spotless. Make sure it stays that way. Every day my wife Sapphire will come down and inspect it. Chores for you boys will be posted on the refrigerator." He said.

The boys sort of sided eyed each other. The look in their eyes summed up what they were thinking. Despite their thoughts, they kept a blank look on their faces.

Floyd was mild compared to what they had heard at the hall.

"After Sapphire approves your chores, you'll be paid $5 a week, another $5 for allowance, and $50 a month for working the grounds. Check your top draw to see where your assignments will be. Work starts at 8am sharp. Don't be late." He said. "Well, I'll let you boys settle in. Supper's at 5:30." He said, and walked away.

One by one they put away their belongings. And one by one, they migrated out to the patio. Jacob's face was still red from being told that he had to get rid of his smokes. Seven dollars he had paid for those smokes, and he was pissed that he had to abandon them.

"You know you could get rid of your smokes on line." Caleb said.

"Yeah, right," Jacob was still seething.

"Like who wants a pack of opened smokes," he said.

"No, I'm serious man. A dude I was at the hall with used to steal smokes from some of the guys, and go on line and sell them. He made pretty good off of it." Caleb said.

"I know that's right." Ezekiel smiled. "At the hall I was at, dudes did it all the time."

"Really," Jacob said.

"Damn man, what hall were you posted up at?" Ezekiel said.

"Some joint up in Las Vegas," he said. "I don't even remember the name of that dump."

"Vegas," Ezekiel replied. "Man, I'd of never left there. And when my time was up, shoot, I'd of found a job at one of them casinos and hit a damn jackpot or something."

"I hear you." Caleb agreed. "It's all kinds of stuff to do out there."

"For real," Ezekiel said. "I was at Coleman; way out in the boonies in Blythe. I always got in trouble until I discovered John Grisham." He grinned. "Cat knows how to tell a story."

"Well, I'm sure you didn't go to the hall for being a book worm." Jacob snickered.

"No punk, "Ezekiel said. "I got caught stealing cars, and one of the dudes just happened to be an undercover cop." He snickered, but it was nervous giggling. "I was trying to get initiated into the gang. When I got caught, they bailed." He shook his head. "Some brother's they turned out to be. So, what about you man?" He asked Jacob.

"Arson," Jacob laughed; thinking it was funny for some reason.

"What the hell?" Caleb said. "Do us a favor, don't act a fool and burn this place down." He laughed.

"That's what I'm saying," Ezekiel said. "What were you pissed about that made you burn stuff up?"

For a minute, the world had stopped for Jacob. He looked at Ezekiel like he needed that question to be asked. But, it never was. In his native orphanage in Russia, he was just a sad depressed child who wanted his parents. To his family in America that adopted him, he was mentally unbalanced, and to the clergymen at his parent's church, he was a devil. Until Ezekiel had asked him, nobody wanted to hear his reason. No one felt he was worthy and neither did he.

"Well," Ezekiel said.

"Well what," Jacob dodge the question, and looked toward Caleb. "So, what about you man?"

"Talking about dodging a bullet," Caleb said. "That was slick," he shook his head. "It was armed robbery." His eyes displayed shame. "I was tired of not having things; tired of struggling; tired of being hungry." He sighed.

"So, my boys and me, we'd rob a bank, split the goods." He said. "It worked for a while, then it ended."

"What happened?" Jacob and Ezekiel said.

"I chose the wrong day and the wrong bank." He remembered it as if it were yesterday. "A plain clothes FBI Agent just happened to be in the bank that day. We didn't know it then, but this guy was trained specifically for our type of crime. We went in like we always did; I gave the note to the teller. This cop must have read her eyes or something. And that was all she wrote."

"Damn!" Jacob said.

"What happened to the other two guys?" Ezekiel asked.

"One was killed, and my brother received fifteen years in prison, and I got sent to the hall at Trenton, in Oakland for five years. But because of good behavior, the state suspended the last year of my sentence so here I am."

The phone rung inside of the house. It surprised them, and for a moment they all sat dumbfounded. Ezekiel finally got up and answered it not knowing if he was supposed to, but he did.

"Hello," he said.

"Thank God." Sapphire said. "Didn't think you boys were gonna answer; thought I was going to have to come down there."

"Didn't know I was supposed to answer," he said. "Floyd didn't mention it."

"That husband of mines," she said. "Yes, you can answer it and use it. Anyhow, wash up, and head over for supper."

"Okay," he said, and hung up. "Hey," he slid open the side door. "Mrs. Sapphire says it's time to wash up for dinner and head on over."

"Okay," they said. They left the patio, washed up, and walked over to the main house.

They could smell the food long before they entered the house. As they entered and sat at the long dining room table, Floyd blessed the meal. The men and young men helped themselves to smothered potatoes, roast chicken, sweet white corn on the Cobb, and macaroni and cheese.

"This is awfully good Mrs. Sapphire." Ezekiel said. "Haven't had home cooking like this since my granny passed."

"You welcome." She said. "So sorry to hear about your granny," she said.

"It was a long time ago." Ezekiel said.

Briefly his eyes showed sadness. He was eight when his grandmother died. And when she died, a part of him died too. She made him breakfast every morning he went to school when his father was passed out somewhere at some crack house. She left work early to pick him up from school, and she sat with him at the kitchen table helping him with his homework. Then, she got sick and passed away. He got angry and gave up on life.

Jacob wiped his mouth, and silently burped. He looked at Sapphire and said in his thick usual accent. "This is really, really good."

"Yeah it is," Caleb said.

"It's plenty more where that came from." She said.

"Hope you all work as hard as you eat?" Samuel wiped his mouth, then drank a glass of sweet tea.

A cruel silence hit the table. The kind hearted little boys that had been lost in their childhood surfaced in their eyes. Jacob's silver spoon smacked the plate hard. He threw his chair under the table and stormed out of the door.

Sapphire's complexion changed. Floyd could tell by his wife's demeanor that Sam was about to become the new main course. Floyd looked down toward Sam and said. "I believe you owe these boys and the boy who left an apology."

Sam looked at Floyd, then looked at the boys. "No harm meant," he said, but his eyes didn't mean it.

Caleb wiped his mouth with his napkin. "It's okay." He said.

"No it's not," Ezekiel replied. "You ain't got no right to be judging me, Jacob, or him. You don't know us man. We ain't done nothing to you, and you need to chill out." Ezekiel wiped his hands, thanked Sapphire and Floyd. "Come on man," he said to Caleb. Caleb thanked them and walked out of the door.

Sapphire stood, threw her napkin on her plate, and placed her hand on her hip. "What right do you have in judging those boys?"

"I said I was sorry." His eyes were grumpy and sad.

"But you didn't mean it. Don't take a fool to know that," she sighed.

"You work here Sam, but you don't own this place. And it's not your place to act like you do." She said.

"If you don't like what my husband is trying to do here, perhaps living with your daughter in Chicago is a better fit for you." She said. Sam's eyes watered and he left the house gloomy.

"Baby," Floyd said.

"Don't," she said. "I know we promised Mrs. Lilly but…"

"He misses his wife. He was with that woman for sixty-seven years, and he doesn't know how to handle it. I know that he can be over the top at times, but in spite of it all, we need to be kind to him. He needs us." Floyd said.

"Floyd Winfrey," she said. "You got a heart the size of Texas, and that's what I fell in love with." She kissed him.

Jacob sat in the backyard tossing small rocks into the still lake. He hated the old man like he hated his parents who had left him at the orphanage and never came back for him. Caleb and Ezekiel came out back and sat with him. They were quiet at first, then Ezekiel broke the silence.

"I checked that fool after you left man." Ezekiel said.

"Floyd got on him to and made him apologize." Caleb put his cap back on his head.

"Exactly," Jacob said, "made him apologize." He shook his head. "Old bastard's been at me before I even got here, and now that I'm here, it's not going to stop." His eyes were frustrated. "This arrangement is not going to work."

"Man, don't do anything stupid." Caleb said.

"Yeah man, just work your program and get the hell out of here." Ezekiel agreed with Caleb.

"My program is nine months." Jacob stood frustrated. "That's the rest of this year, and half of next year, and" he kicked the chair next to him. "There is no way in the hell that I'm going to stay here that long with that old fart treating me like I'm nothing."

"Man…"

"Man nothing," Jacob stared at Caleb. "Maybe you never had anybody hate you so much that they dropped you off at a foreign place where other misfits live, and never came back to get you." Jacob's eyes watered. "Don't you get it? We're misfit's man, and they're not giving a damn about us." He said, as his bottom lip trembled. "We're here because of the money. We screw up and the system gets paid for it. Well, I'm done. You hear me, I'm done!" Jacob stormed off to his room and slammed the door.

Ezekiel and Caleb sat stunned. Their faces were blank and a hollow look stood on them. Caleb stood, and Jacob's pain stood with him. As if Ezekiel could read his mind, "Don't do it man. He needs to cool off. Give him some space."

"I feel it man." Caleb began to pace around in the backyard. "He's going to do something stupid. I feel it man."

"It'll be on him if he does." Ezekiel said.

"Man don't you get it? Didn't you just hear what he said? He's never had anybody." He shook his head. "His parents left him at the orphanage and never came back for him." Caleb stopped pacing and looked at Ezekiel.

"He ain't the only one that's been left man." Ezekiel said. "My old man would binge for days, weeks at a time. I was invisible to him. He didn't even know I was there." He remembered it as if it were yesterday. "Nothing I could do made him see me, or love me. So, I joined a gang thinking I could get from them what I couldn't get from my pop." He shook his head. "They turned on me, but I'm over it."

"Really," Caleb said.

"Yeah," he said. "What the hell is that supposed to mean?"

"Don't play yourself like that man; you're still hurting." Caleb said.

"I don't need nobody. I got me. Unlike that fool in there, I'm gonna work my program and let Vegas get to know EZ." He snickered.

"What about you getting to know you, and learning to give a damn about your brother man?" Caleb left the patio and entered his room.

"Fool ain't my brother," He said tossing a rock into the lake.

A chill had set into the air. Ezekiel's bare legs and arms were unprepared to handle the stiff chill in the night air. He left the patio, entered his room briefly, gathered his pajamas and took a nice hot shower to warm up his chilly bones. He turned his radio on and listened to his listen and relax station. Before he knew it, he had rolled over on his side and went to sleep.

Jacob lay across his bed for hours waiting for the guys to go to sleep. He placed an ear on the wall and he could hear the silence of someone sleeping. On the other side of his bed, was the wall connected to Caleb's room.

Again, he placed his ear to the wall, and like with Ezekiel he heard the sound of sleep.  The long wait was over and the house was still.

Jacob lifted his body from his bed quietly.  He made his bed, cleared his draws, and packed his duffel bag.  He paused at the door; knots in his stomach, and fear lingering inside his throat.  He eased the door open, placed his bag on his shoulder, and walked briskly down the hall.  Jacob strutted through the living room and exited through the side door from the kitchen and ran down to the boat.

Caleb had awakened to a dry throat that needed water.  He sat on the side of his bed for a moment, glimpsing the clock at 4:02am.  He slipped on his house slippers, and opened his door, left his bedroom and entered the kitchen.  He grabbed a glass from the top cabinet, poured himself a glass of water and drunk until the glass of water was gone.  As he sat the picture back into the refrigerator, he noticed the sliding door was opened.  He closed it, and locked it, and then he heard a strange noise.

He pulled back the curtains not seeing anything at first, and then he happened to look towards the lake and saw Jacob tugging at the boat.  "Jacob!"  He yelled.  "Jacob!"

In Ezekiel's sleep, he heard him. He leaped out of bed, and threw open his door. Ezekiel sprinted out of his room and saw that the side door that led to the patio at the kitchen was wide open. He rushed through it and raced down to the lake.

"Jacob," Caleb said. "Jake don't do this man. Let me help you."

"I don't need your help." Jacob said. "And, I don't want it." He continued tugging at the rope to try and loosen the boat from the dock.

"Well, we need yours man." Ezekiel said. "Come on man, it don't have to be like this."

Caleb looked at Ezekiel in shock. Earlier today, he had made it clear that he was going to work his program, and that if Jacob didn't, oh well, that wasn't his problem. He wondered in such a short time what had happened.

"I know that you've never felt like you've had anyone, and I know that you're afraid to trust anything or anyone. But so am I and so is Ezekiel. Come on man, give us a chance." Caleb said.

"Yeah man, reach out and touch. It's cold out here." Ezekiel said. "You have to start trusting somebody, might as well be us."

Jacob wept profusely in the boat and at first it seemed that everything had gone wrong. Floyd had heard the barking of his dogs going crazy, and the commotion of youths yelling. He could only imagine what was going on. He threw on his robe, grabbed his flash light and shotgun and left the main house. Sam hearing the same commotion, grabbed his baseball bat, and rushed as fast as he could old man style in the direction of the noise.

He knew what it was; at least he assumed he knew what it was. Unappreciative boy's trying to escape by boat by the lake. Life had scared them, and they were resorting to what they knew. Maybe Floyd would get it this time? Maybe?

"You have to let me do this my way." Jacob said. "You had no right to interfere."

"What the hell is going on here?" Sam said. "See, I..." Floyd put a hand up as he watched the boys.

What Sam had said didn't even register to the boy's. They were focused on stopping Jacob from making a tragic mistake. Sapphire had joined Floyd's side even though he had told her to stay in the house and wait for him; as if she had ever listened to him.

"Thought I told you to stay put," he said.

"What is going on out here?" She said, as if she didn't hear what he said.

Ezekiel and Caleb stretched out their hands trying to talk Jacob into surrendering, but he was stubborn at first. But, they were persistent, and the two of them kept talking to him. The more they talked, the more they got to him.

"Come on man, take my hand." Caleb said.

"Why? Why should I trust you?" Jacob wept.

"Because we're your brother's man," Caleb said.

Jacob pulled both of them into the boat, and all three boys embraced each other. Sapphire broke down and wept. Floyd placed an arm around her, and tears dripped down his checks like a waterfall. Sam's mouth dropped, and his feeble body seemed too weakened, and he felt like he was going to fall. Instead of his body finding its way to the ground, it was his bat. His icy demeanor melted, and the animosity he had once felt towards the boys had left, and in a compromising moment, he became a brother too.

The End

# Game Change

I was told that mama went into labor with me on the fifty yard line, and that I was literally born in the end zone. That would explain a lot; my love for the game, and this crazy passion that I have for it. I grew up a football brat. I attended the draft before I could crawl, and I paraded daddy's sidelines before I could walk.

That's how it was in the Winslow household; at least it was for me. My older brother Kaleb was different. He liked football, even lettered in it in high school. But, basketball was his first love. And, as good as my dad was at coaching football, Kaleb was as great of a basketball player. He was magic to watch.

The sports bug never seemed to have caught our mother. But, she never missed any of Kaleb's games, or my dance competitions, or any of daddy's home games for that matter. Till this day, I don't understand how she did it. Mama was a busy lady with a huge job. She was a State Supreme Court Justice in California, and she was the Chief Justice of the court. She loved it. Anyone paying attention long enough could tell.

The harder the case, the more her eyes would dance. She was very passionate about law and justice. Daddy however, was passionate about winning football games, especially the big one. He had won four of them, and he was determined to win a fifth.

By the time I was ten, I knew what I wanted to do. At fifteen, I felt I had a solid plan. It seemed perfect. My father was already an NFL coach, four super bowls under his belt, and all the contacts that I would need to make my dream of becoming a coach in the NFL a reality.

At eighteen, my dream hit a brick wall when I poured my heart out to my father at a father daughter lunch we had twice a month at our favorite restaurant, **Dream Big.**

**Dream Big** was a soul food restaurant buffet style. It was owned by a friend of my father, Blue Collins. Blue and my father played together at the University of Alabama. Blue played defense, daddy played offense. To their surprise, they both ended up on the same team, the San Francisco 49ers where they both won two super bowls. Blue paid twelve years, daddy played fifteen. When Blue retired, he built his restaurant, and lived his dream. The rest is history.

I loved the name as much as I did the food. Chicken and dumplings were my favorite. Baby back ribs, greens, black-eyed peas, and a healthy slice of cornbread was daddy's favorite.

**Dream Big** was what I did. Maybe I wouldn't coach the 9ers, but I'd coach some NFL team. I was just eighteen then, and I didn't know my father as well as I thought.

"So, Princess," he licked barbeque sauce from his fingers. "Have we made a decision on those colleges yet that we visited?"

"Stanford maybe," I said, "or maybe the University of Florida?" He paused from eating his ribs, and wiped his mouth first then his hands. By the look in his eyes, I knew that he wasn't pleased. It was as if I sprung on him that I wasn't going to college or something. He placed his elbow on the table, and sighed.

"The University of Florida," he tossed his napkin on the table. "You have got to be kidding."

My mouth was full of chicken and dumplings. I chewed more and swallowed, then drank a few sips of sweet tea. "They have the best sports management program in the country. Minus the hurricanes, Florida is beautiful." I said, and wiped my mouth with a napkin.

He paused again, leaned into the table, nearly getting barbeque sauce on the sleeve of his shirt. "What the hell is sports management, and what happened to going to Harvard, and going to law school?" He shook his head. "Look at what going to Harvard did for your mother."

"Well, I'm not mama, and I don't want to be a lawyer or a judge eventually." I said.

"Well, what do you want to do?" He asked as if he knew that I was going to say something out of the ordinary, and make him crazy. I did.

"I want to be like my father and become a coach in the NFL."

His sleeve suddenly fell prey to the barbeque sauce. His eyes rolled to the back of his head. His complexion changed, and he let me have it.

"Have you lost your mind?" He said, getting more barbeque sauce on his sleeve.

"No," I said. "And, you've got barbeque sauce on your sleeve."

"I don't give a damn about that." He sighed. "I'm trying to figure out how you got this crazy idea in your head? Look around," he said. "Do you see any women coaches in the NFL, or any professional sports for that matter?"

"So," I said. "Jackie Robinson was a first in baseball."

"Jackie Robinson was a man." He smacked his hand on the table hard. "You need to climb out of that fantasy, and come back down to reality and figure something out, because this here is not going to work."

My fork hit the plate. Suddenly my appetite had gone cold. My father's opinion of me made me sick. He single handedly groomed me into a football junkie. He taught me everything I knew about the game, the draft, trades, you name it. If he knew it, I knew it.

"That's a heck of thing for you to say to me." Tears arose in my eyes and my voice started to crack. "You groomed me for this. And, because you decided my gender, suddenly I can't do this." I said. "Well, let me tell you what I won't do." Tears rushed down my face. "I won't go to Harvard. I won't become a lawyer, and I won't let you crush my dreams." I tossed the chair hard into the table and left.

Blue looked over at our table. A worried look stood in his eyes. He watched me storm out of the restaurant, and watched my father push his plate aside; something he'd never done. I didn't speak to my father at all after that. When we took pictures at my high school graduation, I was at the far end, standing next to my brother Kaleb.

When he told me how proud he was of me, I didn't even look at him. And when he tried to hug me, I walked away. Truth be told, I chose Harvard because it was far away from him. Riley Culpepper, the best quarterback that daddy's team the Quakes have ever had, encouraged me to put some distance between my father and I. I felt he was right, so I did.

As quiet as it's kept, I had a mad crush on Riley. And so did every other woman in many different states. Riley was very handsome, caramel skin, coffee colored eyes, and cold black hair cut close to his head that had sort of a wavy wet look to it. I was always finding ways to get around him. I loved looking at him, his muscular arms, buffed chest, and sexy strong thighs that I fantasized about sitting on.

I was under the watchful eye of my father mind you. So, I had to make communication with Riley count. I always made sure that it came directly from daddy; so if he said anything at all I could put it back on him. In a weird way, I got to know Riley pretty well. He noticed the distance between my father and I, and he asked me about it. That's when I confessed, and let the cat out of the bag.

Somehow my ambitious dream of becoming a coach in the NFL didn't rattle him like it did my father. However, it did surprise him. He said he thought that I'd probably go into sports medicine or something.

But, he said that if any female could coach an NFL team, I'd be the one to do it, and to break the barrier. How come Daddy couldn't see me like that?

The pounding on my front door jarred me back from the past, and forced me into the now. I signed out of my journal, locked it, and briskly walked to the door.

"Coming, coming," I said.

"Girl," Sandal said. "You got a man up in there?"

"No," I laughed, letting Sandal in.

Sandal's mother had given her the name after she went into labor at a shoe store and didn't have the chance to purchase the shoes she wanted. Sandal was from the west side of Chicago. Her mother Cheryl owned her own salon, and her father was a detective at the Chicago Police Department.

Like my father, Sandal's father wasn't crazy about her getting into the legal field, but her mind was made up. Unlike my father, he supported her.

"What the hell were you doing?" Sandal said.

"Ah, some research," I lied. "I guess I didn't hear you."

"You think," she teased. "Lunch," she sat hot Philly steak sandwiches on my kitchen table.

"What," I said.

"Maybe that's what I should be asking you?" Sandal said. "Are you okay?" Sandal asked.

"I'm fine." I said. "I don't know why everybody keeps asking me that."

"Maybe it's because the only one you're fooling is yourself." Sandal bit into her sandwich.

"Whatever," I said.

"When's the last time you've been home to visit your folks?" She asked.

"I'm busy you know that, and I talked to my mother just yesterday. And, I talk to my brother every day." I bit into my sandwich.

"What about you dad," Sandal sipped lemon aid. "When's the last time you've seen him?"

"So, how's your man search going, I mean job search?" I snickered.

"Shut up." Sandal had to laugh. "I mean is it that obvious?" She wiped her mouth. "Never mind, don't answer that," she giggled. "But, to answer your question like you've refused to answer mine, I've got my heart sat on living in New York after we graduate." She Said. "What about you?"

"I don't know?" I said. Sandal could see the sadness in my eyes. "I guess I haven't given it that much thought."

"Kye," Sandal set next to me. "You are the brightest, and the best at what you do. Harvard has not seen the likes of you in decades." She said.

"Girl," Sandal looked at me. "I envy you, and so does the rest of our class. I'm just bold enough to say it." Sandal laughed. "You know what I don't get," she sighed. "How could you be so magnificent at something that you absolutely have no interest in at all?"

I looked at Sandal for a moment. The truth had been simmering in my stomach for years. Every time it crept up from the darkest corners of my soul and eased its way into my voice box, I'd force it back down deeper, and it would have to make the slow climb back up.

"I guess I'm angry because my dream died years ago, and it just comes out through this law stuff." I said.

"Well resurrect it and live it whatever it is."
Sandal took another bite of her sandwich.

"It's not that easy." I dipped my fries into ketchup.

"Nothing good ever is," Sandal drunk more of her lemon aid. "But you have to try," she paused briefly. "You'd hate yourself if you suddenly died today, and someone else did what you were born to do."

"Shut up and eat." I ate more of my sandwich and fries.

"Hit a nerve didn't I?" Sandal finished her meal.

"Yeah," I said. "And, if you don't mind I don't want to talk about this anymore."

"Fine, but you know you're going to break down eventually and tell me what it is." Sandal laughed.

The phone rung and I wiped my hands on my napkin and answered it on the second ring. Sandal's eyes were curious as she scooted her chair closer to mines to attempt to hear who was on the other end of the phone. She couldn't make out the voice; couldn't tell if it were male or female. But, by my expression, the smile in my eyes and face, said something and she wanted to know what?

"So, what made you want to talk after all these years?" I asked the person on the other end of the line.

"I can't live with myself anymore, and it's time for the truth to come out." He said.
"I'm visiting my sister in Columbus Ohio. Get to me before I change my mind."

"I'll fly out this afternoon." I was excited as I took down his information.

"I'll only talk to you." He said, "no one else, I mean it."

"Just me, I promise." I said.

"How the hell did you find me?" He asked.

"Determination," I said. "I'll see you this evening, just me alone, I promise." I said.

I celebrated like I use to; pumped fist, hoping up and down at a football game on my father's sidelines. Sandal stood smiling happy to see life inside of me again.

"What?" Sandal said. "What just happened?"

"I need a favor." I said.

"Anything, just tell me what happened." Sandal said.

"Get your sister to book me a flight to Columbus Ohio now. Mr. Jude is ready to talk."

"What?" Sandal was surprised. "I'm coming with you."

"No, you can't," I said. "He wants me to come alone. He says he'll only talk to me."

"Kye, it could be dangerous. I can't let you do that." She said.

"An innocent man has been locked up for fifteen years. His life has been stripped away from him, and his children have had to grow up without a father. Make the damn reservations and tell the legal center that I got a break in the case." I packed.

A soft tap on my shoulder awakened me. It was a smiling, tall gentleman with coffee colored hair, and tender green eyes looking in my face. I rubbed my eyes, and did a double take.

"I know," he said. "I get that all the time."

"I'm sorry." I sat up. "I've just never seen a male stewardess before." I rubbed my eyes.

"Well, you have now." He winked. "We're about to land...somebodies always gotta be a first."

He pressed the intercom and announced that we were landing and gave instructions. He held my hand as I exited the plane. I looked back at him not knowing why, and to my surprise he waved. I waved back and headed through the tunnel and found myself in the airport at the baggage claim. I stood amongst eager people waiting to claim their luggage.

I spotted my royal blue Samsonite carry-on. And, as I went to take it, a hand of a man picked it up. "You must be Kye?" He said.

"Who are you, and how do you know my name?" My look was weird.

"I'm the man you hunted down like a bloodhound and found." He sported a half smile.

"Mr. Jude," I was shocked.

"Call me Ferris," he said. "I've got my truck waiting and my sisters' prepared dinner for us."

We walked a short distance to the parking lot. His silver F-150 was parked in a handicap spot. I noticed he walked with a limp. He sat my bags in the back, and opened my side of the truck, and closed it behind me.

"How'd you know it was me?" I asked.

"Lucky guess," he shrugged his shoulders. "I watched a many of people over at the baggage claim, and..."

"And what, you just took a lucky guess it was me?" I said. "You don't have land to sale me, and my guess is you didn't fall off a turnip truck." I turned looking at him. "You did your research, and you found a picture of me. Nobody gets that lucky." I said.

Ferris had to laugh. I was right. He had found information about the Spencer case, and there were pictures of all the lawyer's and staff associated with the case.

I'm sure my mug shot showed up in there somewhere.

"You are going to make one hell of an attorney." He turned into his sisters' driveway.

"We'll see." I said, as he opened up my door.

"Thanks for coming alone. Now I really know I can trust you." He said.

"It's who I am." I said, as we entered the modest one story house.

The moment I hit the door, I smelt fresh baked bread and chicken and dumplings. It was like I was destined to be there. Ferris introduced me to his younger sister Evelyn. We shook hands, smiled at each other, and she guided us both to the dining area. "I hope you like Chicken and dumplings."

"It's my favorite." I said. "Thank you for having me."

"No," she sat the fresh bread on the table and a large pot of dumplings. "Thank you. I've been at him for years to tell the truth. It's time."

Ferris didn't say a word. He blessed the food. We served ourselves and began eating. We all talked for a while getting to know each other a little. I actually laughed. It felt good. I hadn't done that in years. I had stopped laughing at **Dream Big** seven years ago when daddy killed my dream.

I was stuffed and though I wanted a piece of Evelyn's homemade peach pie, I didn't have the room. I offered to help Evelyn clear the table, but she wouldn't hear of it. She left us to talk. Ferris took his pie to the family room where he divulged fifteen years of pain.

"There's only one way to say this." He sliced a piece of pie with his fork. "My cousin Bobby Kent killed that girl, and his father, my uncle, covered it all up." He said, handing me a thick manila folder.

Bobby Kent at the time had just been picked up by the Kansas City Royals. It had made the tiny Sentinel Press, and the whole town of Wyatt, Colorado was proud. When eighteen year old Megan Cross was murdered, Josh Spencer became an easy target. Josh drunk way too much, listened way too little, and most of the time he woke up in bizarre places or in strange ladies beds. This time he had been accused of killing a young woman he didn't even know.

Bottom line, Sheriff Kent was up for re-election, and his son Bobby had just signed a contract with the Royals. The family wanted answers. The town wanted answers, and Sheriff Kent wanted to be elected again, and wanted his boy to live his dream at any cost. Ferris and the others were forced to keep quiet or else. So, for fifteen years, he kept his mouth shut until now.

Ferris wept hard. In fact, in all my twenty-five years, I've never seen a man weep like that. My heart broke at his sobbing. He cried so much that his tears leaked on his peach pie, and it started to turn soggy. He shocked me so bad. I didn't know what to do.

Before I knew it, I was patting his shoulder trying to console him. His pain was deep and it pulled and tugged at my heart. Now, I was wondering what he had lost in all those fifteen years. It seemed Josh Spencer wasn't the only one who had lost something.

Evelyn insisted that I stay at her home rather than the hotel and I agreed. I combed through every bit of the evidence; talked to every single person that the then Sheriff Kent wouldn't, or threatened like he had his own nephew to keep quiet. I had gotten sworn affidavits from them all. I knew from what I had that Josh was coming home. Hopefully he still had an ounce of hope to resurrect his dreams whatever they were?

I had returned home, or at least what had been home to me for three years. I was meeting with the head attorney over Josh's case and he was pissed to say the least. Sandal had tipped me off so I was prepared for a good cussing out. Sandal was on the hot seat because of me. I felt bad that I had involved her. But, I knew that I had something. I knew that it was a narrow window and that if I didn't jump through it Josh Spencer was done. If it got me kicked out of Harvard Law, it was worth it.

I wasn't in the legal center for two seconds before professor Stillwell and the head attorney over the Spencer case had asked me to come into his office. He was past mad at me. I could tell by the way he rolled his eyes and how he dealt with me.

"Get the hell in my office Kye." He said.

"I can explain." I said.

"Oh really," he slammed the folder that I had given him on his desk hard. "You don't put yourself in a position to where you compromise a case."

"He said he'd only talk to me. What was I supposed to do?"

"Contact me." He said. "Contact me damn it." He sighed. "You're lucky this is good stuff, or..."

"Or what," I became angry. "You'll kick me out of law school. Well go ahead, you'd be doing me a favor. I did what I had to do."

He was stunned, as stunned as I was in saying it. I was tired of living a lie. Truth be told, the only thing that kept me going and kept me in law school was the Spencer case. Josh Spencer's life was taken from him and my dream had been taken from me. I needed to save him with the slightest hope that I could save me.

"I'm going to take that as your blowing off steam.  Besides, you're the best young attorney we've got here."  He said.

"I'm not a lawyer yet."  I said.

"Well, the bar says so, congratulations."  He said.

I was stunned.  I had taken the bar in between research of the Spencer case.  I didn't expect to pass it.  Things changed promptly for me after that.  Josh's case was over turned and he was granted his freedom.

After fifteen years of bondage, he could breathe freedom.  He could hug his boys who had grown up.  He could hold his wife who hung on to hope, and her faith, and believed in Josh when even he had given up.  Beyond the tears in his life was hope; a whole lot of it.  His case made the news everywhere.  And, my face and name went viral.

The offers came pouring in. Before and after graduation, I received many offers. I almost took the job in San Diego, but my older brother Kaleb was always in my ear. My brother Kaleb had flown back to Cambridge to see me so I thought. But what I didn't know was that he had an angle.

Apparently, there was an opening with his pro basketball club as a senior legal counsel. It wasn't bad. It was sports, not football. Nowhere close to being on the sidelines, but was as close to the game as I was probably going to get. But, I wasn't feeling it.

"I don't know Kaleb?" I said, "sounds boring to me."

"Really," he said. "When have sports ever been boring to my little sister?" He stirred my spaghetti sauce. "You'd be negotiating contracts, sports contracts." He tasted it.

"Sis, I'm just trying to help. Let me help you." He said. "This is excellent sauce by the way."

"Maybe you should have gone to law school instead of me." I said.

I had to admit. I did want to go back to California. Kaleb knew me better than anyone, except for my dad. He knew I wanted to come back. And he knew how much I loved sports, and had spent my life being a part of it. He knew very well what he was doing and I caved.

I flew back with him and thought that I was walking into an interview. I didn't. We clicked the moment we shook hands, and the rest is history. I had Kaleb to thank for my new job. At least he brought hope for my dream, and I loved him for it. Again, Kaleb had a slant.

"So," Kaleb bit into a fresh batch of snicker doodles I was making.

"Pop is making dinner for us tonight. He's making your favorite chicken and dumplings." He ate another cookie.

"I can't, work," I said.

It's Saturday." He said.

"And," I fired back.

"And, you're trying to avoid pop." He said.

"It's just easier." I said.

"It's breaking his heart." Kaleb looked at me.

"Well, he broke mines when he killed my dream." I said.

"You can't be mad with him forever." He said.

"He's our dad." He held my face in his hands, kissed my forehead and hugged me.

With Kaleb I could just be a girl. I could cry on his shoulder until I got out whatever was bothering me. That's what I did, I cried a lot and hard.

Dinner was awkward. I hadn't talked to my dad in years, and here I was sitting at their dining room table eating chicken and dumplings. I'm surprised I had an appetite.

But, anger makes you hungry. And I was hungry for something more than dumplings. Daddy stared at me the whole time. He talked football the whole time and all I could say was that's great daddy and little else. Kaleb had eaten my piece of apple pie. I didn't mind. I was full from dinner. Mama smacked his hand, and cut me another slice and placed it in a tuber ware.

I cleared the table. Daddy followed me into the kitchen. He and I both hated awkward silence, so when he followed me into the kitchen, he just said what was on his mind.

"I'm sorry." He said. "I know I hurt you very much that day, and I have lived to regret it ever since."

"All I wanted was for you to believe in me, and you didn't," I said loading the dish washer. "Even if I never got there, even if I never made it, you were supposed to support my dream." I paused and looked at him. "What kind of father destroys his daughter's dream?"

"I'm sorry." He said, tears merging in his eyes. "I just wanted you to be happy." He said.

"Well I'm not daddy, I'm not. But, I can't place all of it on you." I said. "I didn't have to go to Harvard. I didn't have to go to law school." I closed the dish washer door. "The only one I can blame for giving up on what I really wanted is me."

I kissed him on the cheek, took my pie, and dumplings and left. Three days later, I heard the news. Mr. Tisdale was selling the Quakes. Daddy had won four super bowls for him. I knew he would be crushed. Daddy could go anywhere and coach. But, he had built a legacy with the Quakes, and he wanted to end his career there. The news about the sale nearly blew me off my feet. All I could think about was Daddy and what this would do to him.

All the anger I had felt toward my father had left. Besides his family, football was his life. And I felt compelled to do something. This time I gave up my chicken and dumplings and helped daddy eat his baby back ribs. He enjoyed it though he told me to get my own plate.

"Is it true that Mr. Tisdale is selling the team?" I asked.

"Yep," daddy had sadness maneuvering in his eyes. "Says he's tired," daddy paused in plum bewilderment, and disgust. "Truth is baby, old man T has been tired for a while, then I came along and won him four super bowls and the talk of him selling left until now."

"So, you think he'll really sale?" I asked.

"I do. He claims that he's looking for the right buyer. Whatever that means?" He ate another rib.

"What does that mean for you?" I stole a juicy rib.

"I won't coach for another owner. When he sales the team, I'm done." He licked barbeque sauce off his fingers.

"What about your fifth super bowl?" I said.

"Some things just ain't meant to be." He said, and my heart sunk.

I couldn't sleep, couldn't eat, or fully concentrate at work. I couldn't get the look of my dad's face off of my mind; then my miracle came. The Dunbar brother's, the owners of the Kings pro basketball team who my brother Kaleb played for, suddenly decided that they wanted to purchase Mr. Tisdale's football team. Gary, the younger brother was an avid football fan, and he buzzed me to come to his office.

I knew what he wanted and I had my own perspective going in. It was obvious that they wanted me to negotiate the deal and transcribe legal jargon into plain folk talk. Daddy said Mr. Tisdale wanted the right buyer. The right buyer meant somebody who knew the game. Someone that ate it, drank it, breathed it, and slept it. That was me.

But how could I convince either party that I was the right choice? I persuaded Mr. Tisdale to meet me at his stadium. He resisted at first, but he complied. When I arrived, I was standing in the end zone starring down at the place that I was born.

"This is the dam nest thing I've ever agreed to." He shook my hand firmly. "But, there was something in your voice that told me I needed to come here."

"Really," I smiled.

"Really," he smiled back. "I have to tell you." He waved his hand, and like magic two young gentlemen about my age, mid-twenties brought a nice table and comfortable chairs and set it up adjacent to the goal post. "I guess it's possible for folks to have a liking for both sports. But I'm guessing the two Dunbar's are more into this for an investment."

"I suppose people want things for several reasons Mr. Tisdale. I'm just here to represent their interest and try and make this deal." I said.

"But what about your interest, what about your father's interest," he shocked me.

He had caught me off guard, and for a moment, I was tongue tied. I didn't know what to say. I couldn't believe that he remembered me, but I was wrong. He may have been old, but his mind was sharp; sharper than mines at this point. My brain had unthawed, my tongue loosened, and finally, I was able to speak.

"I must say," I said. "I'm very surprised that you remember me."

"How could I forget?" He laughed. "You were practically born in my end zone for Pete's sake." He waved his hand again and there were drinks, and lunch. "You've got football running through your veins." He said, feasting on my favorite chicken and dumplings.

"I want my father to have that fifth super bowl, or at least have the chance to go for it." I scooped up some of the dumplings and immediately I could tell they were Blue's. "But," I wiped my mouth. "I'm representing the Dunbar's and my father, well, he's already said he won't play for another owner."

"He'll play for you though." He sipped sparkling white wine.

My fork dropped hard on my plate. My eyes widen and my mouth completely dropped. I had to shut my own mouth before a fly flew in it.

"But I'm not buying the team," I said. "I don't have that kind of money."

"But, you have the heart," he ate more dumplings.

"I've been watching you for a very long time." He said. "And your daddy's been exceptionally good to this team, this city, and my family."

He drank more wine. "I'm not selling the team to the Dunbar's. They'd just screw everything up that your father and I have worked hard to build."

"So, you're not going to sell it to them?" I said, hoping that the wine hadn't got to his head.

"No, I am not. God's been good to me, and I've got more money than I'll ever spend. I've thought a lot about this and my mind is made up." He said. "I'm giving the team to you. All I ask is that you do better by it than I did, and give your father the chance at number five." He finished his glass of wine, and I nearly choked.

My dumplings sat cold, and like a chill had run through my body. I shook all over. I cried so much and so hard. I doubt that there were any tears left in me for my lifetime. What had I done to deserve this? The media had a field day at the press conference.

They asked me so many questions that my brain went numb. Thanks to Sandal, I was delivered from the mob, and whisked to serenity and silence.

I didn't know what to make of all of this. I wasn't serious about my studies at Harvard, but no matter how I drug my feet, I excelled. I knew for a fact that I absolutely hated law school there. But when I began to work in the legal center and got introduced to Josh Spence's case, something came alive inside of me. I felt compelled to fight for him. I knew I had to win for him or in some strange way I; Kye Winslow would never win in this life again.

The way I understood myself was that I and my father were in a huge battle. He had stolen my dream and I was going to make him pay through guilt. But I ended up paying a bigger price, I gave up and dropped out of life; and for three years I was miserable. I had accused my father of killing my dream. Truth was, I had focused so much on what he told me that I believed it. Thank God destiny is stronger than anger and unbelief.

Just when I had settled; fate turned everything around for me. Without warning, and no effort at all on my part, I was promoted to something far greater than I could ever have imagined. I became the owner of the very team I had yearned to coach. Now, daddy would have to look at me differently. I was more than the game. I was the glue of the organization, now I would have the final say.

This made me excited. At our first management meeting, I glowed. I sat where Mr. Tisdale once sat. I strutted a ponytail with an official Quake cap, Jersey, and matching yoga pants, and sneakers. The shock still hadn't wore off on the coaching staff, and it would be interesting to see how daddy was going to react. Certainly, he couldn't treat me like his little girl anymore. When he arrived he sat across from me. He cleared his throat, and looked me directly in the eyes and said. "Elbows off the table and, Princess sit up straight."

The End